WHAT THIS MYSTERY IS ABOUT . . .

. . . A mysterious woman in a red scarf ... fingerlings and lunkers ... a riddle written on parchment paper ... a cabin in Spearfish Canyon ... ice cream sundaes ... a big, yellow Cadillac ... lilacs and roses ... an Native American princess ... deadly fireworks ... a medicine bag with a strange ingredient ... café lattes at Common Grounds ... magic tricks ... henna tattoos ... clues hidden in a film school documentary ... a fractured friendship ... lip gloss and mascara ... a dangerous trip to Mt. Rushmore ... chicks who kick ... and a priceless ruby.

PEOPLE THIS MYSTERY IS ABOUT . . .

Rinnah Two Feathers
a 14-year-old Lakota Sioux Indian girl whose summer vacation is about to turn deadly

Tommy Red Hawk
Rinnah's best friend, who wants to spend *this* summer exploring the canyon and learning a few magic tricks

Meagen Paige
Rinnah's other best friend, who's got a new crush, new make-up ... and a new woman in her dad's life

Bill Paige
Meagen's dad, who thought a summer in the Spearfish Canyon would make a wonderful vacation

Sandy Price
The local hospital administrator with tragedy, and a suspicious trip to Europe, in her past

Ben Forrest
Son of a famous Hollywood director. Why has he thrown away a promising career of his own just to live in a remote South Dakota canyon?

Mrs. Lane
The family friend who has agreed to spend the summer in Spearfish—and keep the kids out of danger

Tina Treadwell
Mrs. Lane's hip, new assistant has a not-so-secret boyfriend

Ronnie Black Elk
The tribal medicine man

Katharine Black Elk
The medicine man's granddaughter

Victor Little Horn
The school bully with a score to settle

The Woman in the Red Scarf
A mysterious foreigner who gives Rinnah a secret message

THE CURSE OF THE ROYAL RUBY

a Rinnah Two Feathers mystery

by
RODNEY JOHNSON

illustrations by Jill Thompson

UglyTown
Los Angeles

First Edition

UGLYTOWN AND THE UGLYTOWN COIN LOGO SERVICEMARK REG. U.S. PAT. OFF.

Library of Congress Card Catalog Number: 2002-011498

ISBN: 0-9663473-9-0

Find out more of the mystery: RinnahTwoFeathers.com

Printed in the United States of America

10 9 8 7 6 5 4 3 2 1

LiST OF CHAPTERS

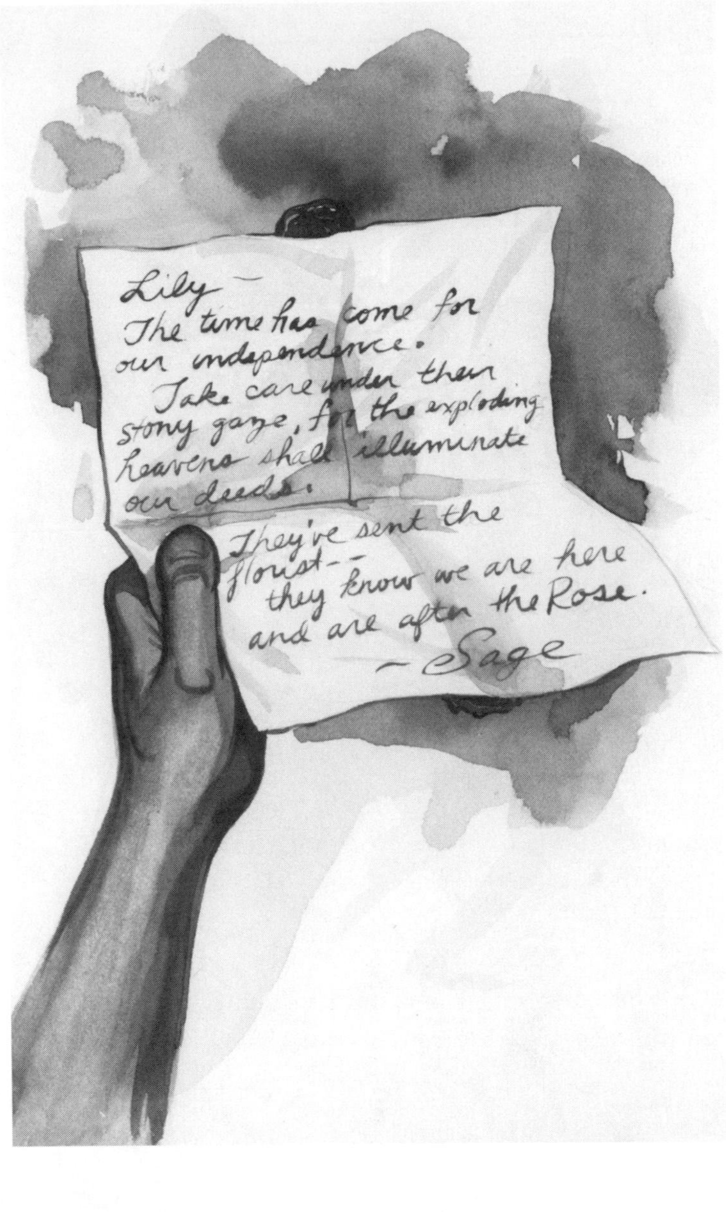
Lily—
The time has come for
our independence.
Take care under their
stony gaze, for the exploding
heavens shall illuminate
our deeds.
They've sent the
florist—
they know we are here
and are after the Rose.
—Sage

A MYSTERIOUS MESSAGE

CHAPTER ONE

RINNAH TWO FEATHERS screamed.

"RUN!"

Her best friend Tommy Red Hawk ran toward her, squinting from the pain that tore through his chest. Someone followed the 14-year-old boy, closing the gap in a furious burst of speed, but Rinnah couldn't quite make out who it was.

With her heart pounding in her chest, Rinnah began to run as well. She pumped her legs hard and felt her blood burn with energy as she hurled her body forward. Without looking back, she sensed that Tommy was catching up to her.

Hurry, Tommy! HURRY!

Rinnah huffed in controlled and measured breaths, her mind focused on the trail that followed a babbling creek. She wore her dark brown hair in one large braid and felt it bounce from shoulder to shoulder with each crashing step. Just ahead, the D.C. Booth Fish Hatchery began to move into view from behind the green, leafy trees that bordered the park.

Rinnah glanced behind her, struggling to remain on the tiny trail. She saw Tommy rounding a curve in the path. She also saw who was behind him, and her heart skipped a beat in its furious pounding. She recognized the acne-ridden face, even now as it contorted in rage and pain. Ralph Standing Deer was mere inches from Tommy and closing fast.

Loser! she thought when she saw the older school bully. She narrowed her eyes and willed her legs to push harder. Suddenly she felt Tommy shove something into her hand. She grasped it tightly and watched from the corner of her eye as her friend ran off the trail and into a thicket of lilac bushes.

Rinnah lunged forward, closer to the edge of the fish hatchery. She spotted Meagen there, hunched over and gaping in absolute terror.

Take it easy, Meagen. We can do this.

Rinnah made eye contact with Meagen and gave a slight nod of her head. Meagen nodded back and began to run.

Hurling herself forward in a final burst of energy, Rinnah sped closer to Meagen. Groups of people lined the trail, and some began to scream. She was just behind Meagen now. She held out her right hand as she continued looking straight ahead. Because she was unable to swing her arm, Rinnah began to slow.

Where is Meagen's hand?

If she didn't pass the baton RIGHT NOW, they would lose valuable seconds in their lead.

Rinnah gave up and used the pumping action of both arms to regain some speed. She was right behind Meagen again and hoped desperately that her nervous friend was ready for the hand off.

Rinnah glanced back, a foolish act at this crucial point in the race, but she had to look. She found Ralph handing off his baton to Leonard White Horse. They were right behind her!

Rinnah snapped her head back around and cried out. "Mea—"

She felt the baton being ripped from her hand. She glanced up and found Meagen grinning as the girl sprinted forward in a mad dash for the finish line just over the bridge and around the corner from an observation deck of the fish hatchery.

Out of breath and thoroughly exhausted, Rinnah slowed to a stop and accepted a paper cup of water from a lady wearing a red baseball cap, one of the volunteers from the Chamber of Commerce here to help out with the "Wild West Days" festivities. She nodded her thanks and wandered over to the observation deck to catch her breath. She reached the platform and found it deserted, the rest of the onlookers choosing to stay at the sidelines for an up-close view of the race. Rinnah walked over to the edge of the deck, where she was just able to see the finish line if she leaned far enough over the railing. She did so and waited for Meagen and Leonard to reach the slash of white chalk that marked the finish.

Even though her heart still pounded in her chest, Rinnah gradually got her breath back. She peered past the many holding pools, some of which were large trough-like containers called raceways that were filled with baby fish, or fingerlings. The deck on which Rinnah now stood overlooked one of the largest ponds and was filled with adult fish. She ignored the large, gray fish now as they bobbed to the surface looking for stale bread crumbs. Instead, she continued to search the finish line with her eyes in an effort to see who would cross it first.

"YESSSS!" Rinnah screamed as she spotted Meagen flying around the corner, two paces ahead of Leonard White Horse. She began to jump up and down, already tasting the victory at hand. Grinning wildly and waving her empty cup in the air, Rinnah saw someone approach her out of the corner of her eye. Another Red Cap, probably to offer more water. Couldn't the lady see she was busy here?

"GO FOR IT, MEAGEN! YOU'RE ALMOST THERE! YOU'RE ALMOST—"

Suddenly, Rinnah felt a hand grip her upper arm. Grip her tightly. She turned to face the Red Cap Lady, ready to tell her that she didn't want any more water, thank you very much.

"Oh!"

Rinnah gasped when she saw that the woman wasn't a Red Cap Lady at all. The woman who stood before her was wearing a bright red scarf wrapped tightly around her head. But it wasn't the scarf that surprised Rinnah so; it was the look in the woman's dark brown eyes as they darted back and forth. The woman glanced quickly behind her and then stared at Rinnah, her mouth open as if to speak.

This lady is really scared of something, Rinnah thought.

The woman's eyes lingered on Rinnah before she finally

spoke. When she did, the words came out in a breathless rush and were tinged with a slight accent.

"They are after the rose!"

Rinnah looked harder at the woman, not sure if she'd heard her correctly. The roar of the crowd as each person cheered was almost deafening, and a flurry of flags, baseball caps and eager hands shimmered brightly in the corner of Rinnah's eyes. She reached up to place her own hand on the woman's arm in an effort to encourage her to repeat herself. But before she could do so, the woman grabbed Rinnah's hand and shoved something into it.

"You understand, no?"

Rinnah gaped and shook her head.

"No. I'm sorry, I don't."

But the woman pressed on.

"You will know. I see it ... inside you. You will help, because you will know. THEY ARE AFTER THE ROSE!"

Rinnah continued to gaze at the woman's eyes and saw something besides fear. What was it? Rinnah took a step closer to the woman and was about to ask her what she meant when the screaming began.

"Aaaaaiiiiyyyy!"

Rinnah jumped nearly out of her skin and whipped around to look in the direction of the frightening wail. She sighed at the sight of Mr. Paige and Mr. Red Hawk holding Meagen high on their shoulders in a victory march. One of the spectators, a local cowboy, was screaming a victory yell, a signal that the race had found its winner.

Rinnah turned back around only to find that the strange woman was no longer there. She walked the length of the observation platform and searched the horde of people milling from pond to pond beneath her. Not seeing a red scarf among the crowd, Rinnah ran to the other end where a stairwell led to the pond's edge. The stairway was empty. She leaned against the railing and looked over the crowd just beyond the pond.

"Where are you?"

As Rinnah continued to search the undulating mass of people, her gaze flitted past a brown stuccoed building that sat at the edge of the platform. Subconsciously, she registered movement in the doorway, but when she looked back, the entrance stood empty. But her memory held a snapshot of a tall figure peering at her from around the heavy wooden frame.

Rinnah took a couple steps toward the building, and read the sign above the door.

"Public Restrooms."

Then Rinnah remembered that the woman had given her something just before running away. She brought her hand up and found a small envelope made of parchment paper. She turned it over and saw that the flap had been sealed with bright-red sealing wax. The seal was broken. Rinnah fingered the wax and felt some kind of design in the center, something she couldn't quite make out. She shifted the envelope in the dappled sunlight for a better view and closed the seal to form the original shape. As a shaft of sunlight hit the wax, she saw clearly what the design was—a single red rose.

Rinnah looked up and scanned the crowd once more. Still no sign of the mysterious woman. She returned her attention to the envelope and frowned as she fingered the wax rose. Finally, she pulled open the flap. She felt more parchment and pulled out a note that had been folded into a crisp square. She opened it and saw that it was a handwritten note. She began reading the words aloud.

Lily -
The time has come for our independence. Take great care under their stony gaze, for the exploding heavens shall illuminate our deeds. They've sent the Florist -- they know we are here and are after the Rose.
    - Sage

Rinnah read the note again, thoroughly confused by its meaning. She looked away from the strange handwriting and gasped.

There, on the other side of the holding pond, stood the mysterious woman. Her scarved head darted back and forth as if looking for something—or someone. She turned and caught Rinnah's curious stare. Her eyes locked on Rinnah for the briefest of moments. Then she slipped behind the visitor's center and disappeared from Rinnah's view.

Rinnah's heart pounded in her chest. She grasped the note tightly in her sweating hand and took a step away from the railing. She looked around, but found herself alone on the observation deck.

"How absolutely unusual!"

THE MEDAL CEREMONY

CHAPTER TWO

"RINNAH! WE DID IT! We won!"

Rinnah had left the observation deck and made her way through the oncoming crowd as it spilled around the different fishponds. Just as she reached the visitor's center, she found Meagen skipping toward her. Not far behind was a red-faced Tommy, hot and struggling to loosen the red bandanna from around his head. Before they got to her, Rinnah slipped the note into the pocket of her shorts.

"What's up with the disappearing act?" Tommy asked. "We were supposed to meet at the finish line, yeah?"

Rinnah looked past Tommy, who finished the cup of water he held in his hand with one loud swallow.

"Something really weird just happened," Rinnah mumbled, almost to herself. But Meagen and Tommy didn't hear as they pulled Rinnah by the arms to get her moving.

"Come on! We have to get over to the stage to accept our medals!" Meagen pleaded, not seeming the least bit tired from her winning dash across the finish line.

Rinnah followed her school chums as they weaved through the crowd, but kept a lookout for the strange woman in the red scarf. She had hoped that the Wild West Days would bring some much-needed excitement to her summer. After all, it wasn't every year that she got to spend her vacation in Spearfish Canyon, where the last weekend in June kicked off a week of events that included a July 4th parade and several fireworks shows—the biggest being held at nearby Mt. Rushmore. But she hadn't expected something so strange as a scared foreigner passing her a bizarre note. And asking for her help.

As they reached the festival area, Rinnah saw many familiar faces from Rosebud, the Sioux reservation that so much of her family still called home. They were here now with booths to showcase their artwork in the form of intricate and colorful beaded moccasins and jewelry. Rinnah's own grandmother was there making traditional frybread and Indian tacos, although her booth was empty just now. She figured that the old woman must have already joined her mother for the medal ceremony.

The three friends headed toward the stage and deeper into the carnival-like atmosphere. Along the way, a familiar friend called to them from somewhere within the crowd.

"There's my adventurous trio! Quick, come stand next to this tree so I can get some shots of the winners!"

Mrs. Lane beamed proudly behind an outlandish pair of huge, pink sunglasses. As she lumbered toward Rinnah and her friends, entire families were jostled to the side by her wonderful girth. She held one hand on top of her head to hold down a huge straw hat and used the other to wave at the kids, the case from her camera dangling like a deflated parachute. Rinnah smiled warmly, not the least bit reluctant to pose for the woman whom she first met when she was a guest at Circle Feather Lodge just over a year ago. In fact, Mrs. Lane had a photo of Rinnah displayed in her Plainsville gallery. It was taken last summer, just after Rinnah and her friends uncovered the secret of Dead Man's Mine.

"Mrs. Lane!" the kids sang in unison. Meagen ran forward and gave the kind woman a firm hug before launching into unnecessary details about the race and its thrilling outcome.

"Sweetheart, I know all about it," Mrs. Lane replied. "I was right there at the finish line and got some excellent shots. I used my new digital camera your father helped me pick out, Meagen."

Mrs. Lane brandished her high-tech toy like it was a holy relic meant to inspire awe and convert heathens. She suddenly gasped dramatically and turned to Rinnah.

"Oh, I almost forgot, Princess. Your mother sent your bag with Tina."

Mrs. Lane bobbed precariously on tiptoes as she scanned the crowd for her new assistant.

"Wherever did she get off to?" she asked as she peered between trees. Just then, a voice sang out from behind her

"Congratulations, guys!"

Mrs. Lane's face lit up as she spotted Tina Treadwell coming from one of the fish holding pools. Strikingly pretty, the 24-year-old's short, black hair was tousled stylishly and showed off three silver hoops in each ear. Black eye-liner accentuated the exotic shape of her dark, gray eyes and a black lace blouse completed the cool, hip look the girl exuded without a second thought. Rinnah had often wondered if she would keep her bohemian look now that she had finished graduate school. Of course, with a degree in art history, she figured that a little urban style might be expected when working in the art world. As it was, Mrs. Lane found her "a delight" and had hired her immediately as a summer intern.

As Tina gave the kids a thumbs-up for winning the race, Rinnah noticed an intricate design on the top of her right hand. Over the hand and down her fingers, an intricate lace of burnt orange stained the skin like a jeweled glove.

"That's new," Rinnah said pointing to Tina's hand.

"It's henna," she explained. "That stuff they draw on your skin like a fake tattoo." She held the hand up for closer inspection. "I came out this morning and had it done at one of the booths. Cool, huh?"

Rinnah and Meagen answered with enthusiastic nods as Tina removed Rinnah's backpack and handed it to her.

"We should hurry," Mrs. Lane clucked as she waved the camera over her head. "Your parents are expecting you at the medal ceremony."

While Tommy and Meagen positioned themselves around a tree with practiced precision, Rinnah removed the parchment from her pocket and slipped it into her backpack. Finally, after a few more pictures for Mrs. Lane, the gang proceeded on to the ceremony without further interruption.

"Now, you kids run on ahead. You don't want to miss your medals. We'll be with your parents in the audience,"

Mrs. Lane said as she put away her camera. "Try to find me, so I can get some good pictures!"

Mrs. Lane, followed by her assistant, lumbered off toward the festival seating area, humming loudly and smiling at strangers as she went.

The awards ceremony felt a little hokey to Rinnah, but she enjoyed it anyway, especially when she spied Ralph Standing Deer pouting at the edge of the stage. Just as Rinnah made her way back from accepting her medal, she scanned the crowd and spotted a familiar smirk.

Victor Little Horn stood next to his friend Ralph and puffed delinquently on a cigarette. His shoulder-length black hair blew in his eyes, and when he pulled it away from his face, Rinnah noticed a new tattoo on his bicep. Even from the stage, she could make out the feathers of a war bonnet done in black ink.

"Omigod!" Meagen gasped when she spied the gang's old enemy. "He's so ... *different!*"

Rinnah shrugged, not taking her eyes away from the older boy. "So he grew a couple inches," she said.

Meagen turned her face slowly toward Rinnah and cocked a plucked eyebrow. "*A few inches?*" Meagen repeated. "Please! He's gotten so tall it's like ... weird."

Indeed, Victor Little Horn had grown like a prairie

weed in the past year. The boy was close to six feet tall now, making him the tallest 16-year-old in three counties. Rinnah herself had grown a few inches since she had her last conversation with the school bully. When her 14th birthday hit last August, she secretly began to chart her growth spurts, using the inside of her bathroom door jam. As of this morning, she was up to 5' 4". Even Meagen had grown, and seemed neck-and-neck with Rinnah in the tallness category. Tommy, unfortunately, was another story. It was an unspoken agreement between Rinnah and Meagen not to discuss it with him. They all knew it was just a matter of time before Tommy shot up with the rest of them.

Rinnah tried to remember when that last conversation with Victor was. Then it hit her. Last summer at Chief Running Bear's funeral. Victor was there with his father and avoided Rinnah like first period gym class until she cornered him at the gravesite. All she could get out of him was an awkward "Thanks" for clearing his name at school. But anger clung to him like fur to a bear and Rinnah wondered what it would take to shed it from his soul once and for all. Tommy had been surprised that Victor wasn't in jail for his part in last summer's mystery, but was later overjoyed when school started and they discovered that Victor had dropped out.

"Shouldn't he be picking up trash on the side of a high-way or something?" Tommy asked.

Meagen stood in front of Tommy in an effort to block his view of Victor. "Lighten up," she said. "He's obviously just here with Ralph."

Tommy stood on his tip-toes in an effort to see past Meagen. Finally, he gave up and looked away.

"I hope this doesn't mean we're going to be seeing him all summer," he said. He then hawked a loogie and wiped his mouth. "We're a hundred miles from home, and we *still* have to put up with that loser?"

Meagen gagged and stepped away from Tommy.

"C'mon, Tommy," Rinnah pleaded, ignoring the loogie-chuck. "It's our first day in the Canyon, and we have a whole six weeks ahead of us. Don't let Victor get to you."

Rinnah hoped that Tommy wouldn't ruin things by going on the warpath. Like Tommy, she was excited about spending the better part of the summer away from Plainsville—and her chores back at Circle Feather Lodge. Helping her mom run a vacation retreat out of their home could some-times spoil her time off from school. She was ecstatic when Meagen's dad told them about the cabin he rented for the summer and invited the kids to join them on vacation. But like Tommy, she was disturbed at the sight of Victor Little Horn just as their vacation was getting started.

"Rinnah's right, Tom," Meagen was saying. "We've got so much planned for this summer that we don't have time to even think about Victor."

Tommy continued glaring as Meagen went on.

"It's been a long time. Maybe playing Construction Guy for his dad all year has changed him."

Tommy finally turned away. He missed seeing Victor smile wickedly and blow a kiss in his direction.

"Or maybe not," Rinnah said.

As she and Meagen caught up with Tommy, Rinnah couldn't help feeling that her summer vacation was taking a very strange turn. First a bizarre encounter with a scared woman and now Victor Little Horn at the Wild West Days.

Rinnah frowned and thought to herself, *what next?*

AN INTRODUCTION AT DIRTY EDDY'S

CHAPTER THREE

WITH THE CEREMONY OVER, the kids regrouped with their parents for a celebration at Dirty Eddy's Ice Cream Saloon in downtown Spearfish. Just as they arrived, Mrs. Lane pulled up in her large yellow Cadillac. She parked the boat at a wild angle in front of the sweet shop.

"We were beginning to think you stood us up," Mr. Paige said with a smile.

"Well, you can blame this one," Mrs. Lane answered with a breathless nod toward Tina. She then winked at her red-faced assistant to show she was just giving her a hard time. "Tina got away from me during the ceremony, and it was all I could do to find her again. The crowds are massive this weekend!"

Mrs. Lane removed a bright pink handkerchief from her bag and dabbed delicately at her moistened brow.

"We'll see if we can't cool you off with some ice cream," Rinnah's mom said as she took the over-heated and over-excited Mrs. Lane by a plump arm.

"Well, if you don't mind too much," Tina said, "Mrs. Lane and I are going to look over some lighting catalogues. We want to get some new spots hung before the summer gets too busy."

Mrs. Lane clucked and shook her head.

"I can't get her to stop working, even for a moment," she said as Tommy held the shop's door open for her. "Will someone please tell her that I can't concentrate when there's hot fudge around?"

Tina chuckled and threw an arm around her boss.

"This won't hurt a bit. I promise."

Reluctantly, Mrs. Lane allowed her assistant to lead her to a small table in the corner of the ice cream parlor.

"Dad!" Tommy called. "I'll be right back, yeah?"

Mr. Red Hawk turned and watched as his son dashed down the sidewalk.

"Where's he going?" he asked.

"The magic shop," Rinnah answered. "He's been dying to buy some of the stuff in there."

Just as Tommy reached the door to "Spearfish Sadie's Magic Shop," he turned and yelled.

"Order me Rocky Road. Triple scoop!"

Mr. Red Hawk waved him off and turned to Rinnah. "I'm not sending him any more money!"

Rinnah giggled and walked into the ice cream parlor.

Soon, everyone was seated around two tables and reading menus with watering mouths. One by one, they gave their ice cream selections to a teenaged boy who responded with a thumbs-up sign after each order. Once Rinnah had a moment to think, she replayed the scene with the strange woman over in her mind as her friends and family chatted around her. She tried to remember if there was anything else about the woman that could help provide some answers as to what she was so afraid of. The way her eyes darted around the fish hatchery, Rinnah was sure that the woman felt she was in some kind of danger. Was someone chasing her? And if so, why?

Then Rinnah thought about the strange note the woman had given her, how the wording of it was so weird. Almost like it was meant to be a puzzle.

As Rinnah thought about it, she came to the conclusion

that the woman must have had to ditch the note, and ditch it fast. That meant that she must have seen someone at the fish hatchery, someone that made her very afraid. And someone who must never read that note, no matter what.

"HAHAHAHAHAHA!"

Rinnah jumped at the sound of Meagen's infectious laugh. She watched as Mr. Paige threw an arm around his daughter and kissed her cheek.

Rinnah shifted in her seat. She missed her own father. But his death had somehow become a more comfortable part of who she was, and who she would become. Now the hurt had faded to something like the memory of a bad sunburn, when the damaged skin had peeled away to reveal a new layer, one that was healthy and no longer raw. These days, Rinnah felt only the occasional tingle from the hot sunshine of her father's memory. Sometimes she would see Meagen with her father and those memories would begin to tingle in her mind all over again. Like now.

"You were so mad at me when we got our new house," Mr. Paige said between fits of laughter.

"Well, duh! I spent Christmas Eve peeling wall paper."

"Oh, so I guess you wanted to stay in that tiny rental house with the cracked windows? Or maybe I should just find Buck Eye a new home. I know he's got to be a lot of work for you."

Meagen gasped in terror, the panic evident in her eyes. Just when Rinnah thought that her friend would implode with anxiety, Mr. Paige winked and kissed his daughter on the forehead.

"That is SO not funny," Meagen said with an unconvincing pout. Just then, Tommy returned with a large, plastic sack bulging with magic supplies.

"I'm getting ready for next year's talent show!"

Meagen reached over the table and peered inside the bag. Tommy snatched it and put it under the table.

"No looking! This is for serious magicians only, yeah?"

Meagen rolled her blue eyes and fell back into her seat. "Whatever!"

Finally, the teenage boy and an older woman wearing a pink apron set large trays of ice cream on the table. A moment of confusion reigned as hands went everywhere, passing ice cream sodas, pineapple sundaes, and frozen yogurt.

Meagen swallowed a heaping spoonful of peach ice cream and asked, "When do Buck Eye and Dancer get here, anyway?"

Mr. Red Hawk wiped his mouth with a pink paper napkin before answering.

"Rinnah's grandfather is getting the trailer cleaned up today, so we'll be bringing the horses out tomorrow."

Rinnah's mom then turned to her daughter. "That reminds me," she said. "You and Meagen need to be extra careful with those horses. The land around here isn't flat like it is back home. It's different riding through the hills. One bad step could be disastrous."

Rinnah sighed. She had heard this lecture about a thousand times since the girls had talked their parents into allowing the horses to join them for the summer. She chose her words carefully.

"Mom, we've already talked about this. We promise to let Mr. Paige know exactly which trails we'll be riding on and when. Besides," she said as she scooped a bright red cherry from her double chocolate milkshake, "Meagen has her cell phone. We'll take it with us."

Mrs. Two Feathers glanced at Meagen's dad. He gave a slight nod and a wink to show that he had it under control.

"All right," she said with a reluctant smile. Then, off Rinnah's eye roll. "I'm the mom. I'm supposed to worry."

Rinnah responded by giving her mom a sticky kiss on the cheek and noticed that Mr. Paige was waving frantically at someone out on the sidewalk. Rinnah looked out the window and saw a tall woman in an elegant summer suit. The lady removed a pair of sunglasses to reveal eyes that looked almost the exact shade of lavender as the suit she wore. She smiled and pushed a stray lock of blonde hair behind her left ear and nodded as Mr. Paige went to the front door.

Rinnah glanced at Meagen, but since the girl had her back to the window she didn't notice the woman out on the sidewalk at all.

Mr. Paige returned to the table with a smile—and a hand on the woman's back.

"Everyone," he said. "I want you all to meet someone."

Meagen glanced up from her melting ice cream and smiled.

"This is Sandy Price. She's the hospital administrator for Spearfish General."

The men stood from their seats and made introductions while Sandy shook hands. When she got to Meagen, Rinnah noticed that the woman smiled even larger than before.

"It's so nice to meet you, Meagen. How did you do in the race today?"

Meagen beamed with pride but Tommy chimed in before she could answer.

"We totally blew them away!"

Meagen giggled and began describing the race as Mr. Paige took an extra chair from a nearby table. When he returned, Sandy was listening intently to Meagen's story and did not immediately notice the chair. Mr. Paige placed his hand on the small of Sandy's back in an effort to let her know that she could sit. But she didn't sit down just then. Instead, she continued standing and listening to Meagen's story. And Mr. Paige's hand lingered on Sandy's back. Finally, Sandy looked behind her and found the chair that Mr. Paige had fetched.

"Oh. Thank you, Bill."

Sandy Price sat down and looked around the table.

"How about some ice cream?" Mrs. Two Feathers asked. As Rinnah's mom began to scan the room for the waitress, Sandy shook her head.

"Oh, nothing for me, thanks," Sandy replied. "I've just come from a working lunch, and I'm stuffed."

As the group chatted with Sandy, Rinnah sneaked a curious peek at Meagen. She was surprised to see her friend joking with Tommy. They were stealing bites of each other's ice cream and laughing. Beside them sat Meagen's father and Sandy Price. Rinnah noticed that Mr. Paige smiled and laughed in a way she had never seen before. Meagen continued playing with Tommy and didn't seem the least bit interested in the conversation going on right next to her.

"She doesn't know…" Rinnah said to herself. She remembered last summer when the truth about Meagen had come out: Her mom had left Meagen and her dad earlier that year. It's why they moved to Plainsville. The fact that Meagen's mom didn't want to have anything to do with them nearly crushed the poor girl. Meagen had come a long way since last summer. Now Rinnah wondered if she had come far enough. Just then, Mrs. Lane walked up to the group.

"Well, we've got to run," she said. "Tina's found a fabulous electrician, and he agreed to meet with us for a moment this afternoon, but I couldn't leave without meeting your lovely new friend, Bill." Mrs. Lane gave Meagen's father a jovial wink, causing him to blush scarlet.

"Oh, gosh! How rude of me," Mr. Paige said as he stood from his chair. It nearly fell over in his haste to rise, but Sandy caught the chair before it clattered to the floor. Meagen raised her eyebrows and watched as her father made introductions.

When Mrs. Lane made to leave, she whispered, quite loudly, "She's just marvelous!" causing Mr. Paige to blush all over again.

Rinnah glanced at Meagen, but found only a brief flicker of confusion pass her eyes before the girl went back to her ice cream. Meanwhile, Sandy engaged Mrs. Two Feathers in friendly chatter.

"Yes, it does get awfully crowded in this little town over the summers," she was saying. "But it's so good for the local economy, as I'm sure you're aware. Bill's told me all about Circle Feather. I would love to see it sometime."

"And we would love to have you," Rinnah's mom answered. "Just as soon as it's settled down a bit, you should come for dinner. Right now, we're booked solid for the next six weeks!"

"I know what you mean. With all the tourists, the hospital is a mad house until the fall. That's when I'm finally able to take some vacation of my own. Like last fall, I spent a wonderful three weeks in Europe. Have you been?"

Rinnah's mom shook her head. "No, but I would love to. My late husband had tried to talk me into it for years, but Rinnah was too young, really, to appreciate it. Now that she's older, I've often thought we should give it a try."

Rinnah perked up at the mention of her name in connection with a trip out of the country. Her mom caught her looking and said, "Maybe a High School graduation present?" She gave Rinnah a wink and Sandy laughed when Rinnah's eyes nearly bulged out of her head.

"We should probably get moving..." Tommy's dad said with a quick look around the table.

Mrs. Two Feathers twisted a beaded watchband around her wrist and glanced at the time. "You're right. It's later than I thought."

Before Rinnah could question her mother's sincerity

about the trip, the sound of chairs scooting away from the table echoed through the ice cream parlor. Mrs. Two Feathers gathered her purse while talking to Rinnah.

"Honey, we need to get your things from the car. And I've got to find your grandmother and get back to Circle Feather before the lodgers starve to death."

Mr. Paige stepped back from the table and made room for Sandy to stand.

"Let's get my Jeep loaded with the kids' luggage so the rest of you can hit the road," he said.

"And I really should be checking on things at the hospital," Sandy explained. "I had to do some fast talking to get our computer guy to come in today and get things ready for Bill. I just want to make sure he doesn't totally hate me." With that, Sandy looked around the table.

"It was so good to meet all of you. I hope I see you again soon."

Meagen wiped her lips with a napkin and waited for Tommy to gather his magic supplies.

"Don't worry," she said when Tommy narrowed his eyes. "I'm not looking."

When Meagen turned around, she found her dad looking at her.

"What?" she asked.

Her dad cocked his head toward Sandy, who was saying

goodbye to Rinnah's mom. Meagen rolled her eyes and stepped forward.

"It was nice to meet you," she said politely when Sandy had turned away from Mrs. Two Feathers.

"And it was great to meet you, Meagen."

Tommy squeezed between the two and went to shake Sandy's hand. He opened his mouth and—

"Buuuuurrrp!"

His hand flew to his mouth and his eyes bulged in shock.

"Sorry," he mumbled.

Sandy laughed and gave him a quick pat on the shoulder. "No harm done, Tommy."

Meagen turned to Tommy and glared.

"That is so rude," she said, and made her way past Sandy and out onto the sidewalk.

The smirk Rinnah gave Tommy faded when they stepped outside.

"Where's everyone going?" she asked as she peered down the street.

Tommy and Meagen followed Rinnah's line of vision and found that many of the tourists were walking away from Main Street. A few of them even began to run.

"It looks like they're all going back to the fish hatchery," Mr. Red Hawk said.

Mrs. Two Feathers grabbed hold of Rinnah's hand to keep her from getting too far away, but quickened her step to keep up. The rest of the group followed them and the crowd of tourists as they made their way to the hatchery.

When they reached the edge of the park, a large crowd had gathered along the railing that circled the largest pond. Rinnah jumped impatiently, trying to get a view of the water just over the wooden fence, but was having no luck in seeing through the crowd. Just to her right was a set of metal steps that led up to a platform. Unfortunately, the area was off limits to tourists, made obvious by a locked iron gate.

"I'll ask someone if they know what's going on," Mr. Red Hawk said as he slipped away from the group and deeper into the throng of onlookers. Rinnah glanced over to the stairway just in time to see Tommy scaling the small gate. With a grin, Rinnah stepped unnoticed away from her mother and followed.

"Wait for me!"

Rinnah looked back over her shoulder as she was climbing the gate and saw Meagen looking flushed and excited.

In just under a minute, all three friends stood perched on the best look-out area of the entire fish hatchery. Looking at the pond 10 feet below them, Rinnah saw the murky, green water filled with some agitated rainbow and brown trout. She also saw two men in tropical print shirts and khaki shorts struggling in the water.

"Looks like they're dragging something," Rinnah half

whispered. She looked harder and gasped when she realized what it was.

"It's a person!" she cried. "Someone must have drowned!"

At that very moment a siren began wailing in the distance, screaming louder as it got closer to the fish hatchery.

The crowd rippled with astonished murmurs as the two good Samaritans got closer to the edge of the pool. Rinnah noticed that one of them let go of the body and waded back out to the deeper part of the pool.

"What's he doing now?" Tommy asked from Rinnah's side.

"He's going back out to get something. See? Something's still in the water."

Rinnah peered even harder over the edge of the platform in an effort to see the floating object. Suddenly, her heart seized as if gripped by an icy fist, and she gasped in horror and recognition.

"Oh my God!"

The man with the tropical shirt fished the object out of the water and held it up to the sun. There, dripping like a bloody flag, hung a bright red scarf.

THE BODY IN THE POND

CHAPTER FOUR

"SHE'S ALIVE. But barely."

Mr. Red Hawk had returned to the group nearly a full hour after he left. Rinnah, Tommy, and Meagen had joined their parents at the same time the ambulance had arrived, and Rinnah was full of questions.

"What happened?" she asked. The strange expression on Mr. Red Hawk's face made Rinnah even more curious. She twisted the end of her braid and leaned in close.

"Well, I overheard the paramedic telling the police that there were signs of a struggle." Mr. Red Hawk gawked uneasily at his feet and Rinnah felt her mother's arms encircle her waist.

"You mean, someone tried to kill her?" Meagen blurted.

Rinnah remembered the look of fear in the woman's eyes as she said those strange words.

"They are after the rose."

"What was that, honey?"

Rinnah looked up to see her mother gazing down at her and realized that she must have repeated that poor woman's words aloud.

"Nothing, Mom. I was just thinking…"

"Well, it's time we left. As it is, we're going to hit a lot of traffic just getting out of the fairgrounds." Rinnah looked around and saw that her mother was right. People stood talking in small groups, while cars circled the block and made their way to the highway in sluggish lanes.

The now-solemn group walked over to the parking lot to find a breathless Mrs. Lane waving at them from between their cars like a deranged airport runway attendant. Behind her followed a distraught looking Tina.

"Mrs. Two Feathers! Mr. Red Hawk! Isn't it just awful?" she cried when the group joined her. "That poor, poor woman. Left for dead in the fish pond!" Mrs. Lane waved a wilted handkerchief in front of her bright red face as Mr. Paige offered his arm for support.

"Yes, we know all about it," he said in a soothing tone. "I'm sure the police will get this straightened out in no time at all. The best thing we can do is leave them to it."

Rinnah threw an arm around Mrs. Lane and with the help of Mr. Paige, guided her through the parking lot until they reached her Cadillac. Tina opened the driver's door and stood to the side as Mrs. Lane landed with a plop into the seat, causing the car to rock violently. Rinnah noticed that Mrs. Lane was beginning to look angry as she sat staring out from behind the steering wheel. She then heard her mother speaking to Mr. Paige in low tones, which immediately put Rinnah on the alert. Trying hard to look inconspicuous, Rinnah took a step toward her mother.

"I'm a little worried about leaving the kids here just now," Rinnah heard her say.

Mr. Paige looked around, his eyes falling upon Rinnah. Rinnah could tell he felt the same way.

No one spoke for a few minutes, and Rinnah found herself thinking about the woman in the fish hatchery. She clutched her bag, remembering the note that she hid there. Those words held some kind of important message. Important enough to fight for. But what?

Rinnah suddenly realized that someone was speaking. She cleared her mind of lingering questions and heard Mrs. Lane talking from the front seat of the car.

"—dreadful! That's what it is. With all the tourists roaming around, no one saw enough for the police to make an immediate arrest. Now there's some lunatic out running around attacking poor, defenseless women in broad daylight!"

Tina merely nodded and patted Mrs. Lane's arm as it hung out the open car window.

Rinnah sensed her mother becoming anxious and knew immediately what was coming.

"Bill ... I think we should wait a while before the kids come and stay in the Canyon. The cabin sounds pretty remote, and, well..."

Just as Rinnah thought. No vacation in the Canyon for her this summer. *Now how will I solve this mystery from all they way out in Plainsville?* she thought to herself. Obviously, Meagen wasn't too thrilled with the idea either. Her pleading eyes burned a hole through her father's head.

"Dad, we're fourteen years old. We can take care of ourselves."

Mr. Paige glanced at Rinnah's mother while he thought about it. Rinnah saw the look in his eyes, and it told her that Meagen was about to get her heart broken.

"Honey, I think Mrs. Two Feathers is right. You know I'll be at the office until very late each evening. I just couldn't let you kids be here alone until the police capture this maniac. It just wouldn't be safe."

Meagen crossed her arms and leaned against the Cadillac. Her face turned bright red, and she looked away. Rinnah could tell that Meagen was beginning to cry, and she wasn't the least bit surprised. They all had been so excited about having a real vacation in the Canyon this summer. The thought of going home made Rinnah feel just as disappointed—but perhaps for slightly different reasons.

Rinnah heard a heavy rustling coming from the front seat of the car. When she glanced at Mrs. Lane, she found the woman looking painfully at Meagen. Suddenly, the woman's eyes lit up, and she clapped her fleshy hands in joy.

"I've got an idea. Why don't I come and stay as well? I could be there for the kids while you're at work."

Meagen, sensing a last minute save, uncrossed her arms and stepped forward. Just as she was about to speak, her father cut her off.

"Mrs. Lane, that just wouldn't be fair. You've finally got your gallery up and running. There's no way I can ask you to come babysit for half the summer."

Meagen fell back against the car as if she had been hit. "*Babysit!* You have *got* to be kidding," she groaned.

"Whatever you want to call it," Mr. Paige continued, ignoring his glowering daughter. "It's too much to ask."

"Don't be so bull-headed, Bill!" Mrs. Lane chided. She then hauled herself out of the car, causing Meagen to step away when it lurched upward. "I have Tina now, and she's a perfectly capable assistant."

With that, all eyes were cast on Mrs. Lane's young assistant.

Tina, looking a little uneasy, tried to make herself invisible by stepping away from the car. But since she was now the center of attention, she spoke up.

"Uh ... sure. I can take care of things back at the gallery. As long as I can reach Mrs. Lane by phone, that is."

"Of course you can, dear," Mrs. Lane answered. Then, to Mr. Paige, "I'm sure this cabin is equipped with the latest technology, such as telephones?"

Mr. Paige nodded reluctantly. "Of course."

"Good!" Mrs. Lane continued. "Besides, the gallery is only open four days a week. And it's a mere two hours away from the Canyon. That's not too far away should I be needed to take care of any emergencies."

Mr. Paige looked doubtful and was about to speak when Mrs. Lane cut him off.

"I know what you're thinking. But let me assure you, Bill, that I wouldn't let anyone so much as touch one tiny hair on the heads of any of my angels without having to go through me first."

She pursed her lips and patted her hair, daring Meagen's dad to contradict her further. Everyone standing around the car knew that under all that make-up, Mrs. Lane was a real bulldog. No one doubted for a second that the kids would be safe while under her care.

"It's all settled," Mrs. Lane declared. She then began giving Tina a list of items that would need immediate packing for her extended stay in the Canyon, as well as instructions to return in her Cadillac tomorrow at the same time Rinnah's grandfather would be coming with the horses. Rinnah caught Mr. Paige smiling and knew that the subject was closed. The vacation was back on!

As the adults discussed details and loaded luggage into Mr. Paige's Jeep, Rinnah began to plan her investigation. The first step was to figure out that note. As she was rummaging in her bag, she felt a hand on her shoulder.

"Oh!"

When Rinnah looked up, she saw an old Native American woman, shorter than herself and wearing a light summer dress. Her long, gray hair flowed around her dark, heavily lined face. Her brown eyes twinkled in the late afternoon sun, and her bone earrings rustled delicately as she moved.

"Hi, Grandmother," Rinnah said. "You scared me."

Her grandmother chuckled musically and absently fingered the quill necklace that circled her throat. Rinnah's jaw ached with the memory of her grandmother teaching her how to make it, the way she spent hours pulling the porcupine quills through her clenched teeth to straighten each quill before threading it on catgut string with cut-glass beads. The result was a traditional necklace worn by nearly all the elders of her tribe, and one day Rinnah would be just as good as her grandmother at making them.

"I was told what happened to the white woman in the fish pond and brought you something you will need in the days ahead." With that, Rinnah's grandmother slipped something over Rinnah's head.

"This medicine bag will protect you. I had Ronnie Black Elk bless it for you."

Rinnah touched the tiny purse made of rawhide and felt the shapes of its sacred contents; a sage leaf, tiny crystals, bits of coyote bone, and a nugget of Black Hills gold. Mr. Black Elk was the medicine man of her tribe and would bless medicine bags like the one she now wore through chanting and prayer.

"He said to tell you that this one is special, for he added something to it. Something just for you, with a power and meaning only you would understand," Rinnah's grand-mother continued.

"What else did he put in here, Grandmother?"
The old woman paused briefly before answering.
"Rose petals."

AN UNEXPECTED VISITOR

CHAPTER FIVE

As the Jeep wound its way through Spearfish Canyon, Tommy and Meagen chatted with excitement about their whole month and a half away from Plainsville. Rinnah, on the other hand, remained quiet. Mrs. Two Feathers had still seemed unsure about letting Rinnah spend so much time away from home, but Mr. Paige did his best to put her mind at ease. She and Rinnah's grandmother finally left for the drive back to Circle Feather, but not before making Rinnah promise to keep in constant communication with Mr. Paige. Her grandmother said nothing more to Rinnah about the medicine bag—or its interesting contents.

Mrs. Lane had made a quick stop in some of the shops to purchase things she would need for her first night away from home. Now, the gang was on their way to the Paiges' rental cabin somewhere deep in the Canyon.

Rinnah silently took stock of her situation from the back seat of the Jeep, one that had changed drastically since learning of the medicine man's message. She felt that greater things were at work here and she must help the foreigner in whatever quest the mysterious woman had embarked upon. Her voice, obscured by the sound of Mrs. Lane rummaging through paper bags from the front seat, Rinnah whispered to her comrades.

"You guys, I've got something to tell you. Something that happened today during the race."

Tommy and Meagen hushed their animated discussion and looked at Rinnah, who sat between them with her bag on her knees. She paused and listened as Mrs. Lane began conferring with Mr. Paige over a grocery list. Satisfied that the grown-ups in the front seat weren't listening, Rinnah continued.

"That woman talked to me while I watched the race. And she seemed pretty scared."

Meagen twisted in her seat to get a better look at Rinnah, stunned by the news.

"You talked to her? About what?"

Rinnah clutched her bag tighter, thinking about the note that she had hidden there.

"I think now that she must have been running from someone. And that someone later tried to kill her."

Tommy's eyes nearly bugged out of his head.

"And you didn't tell the police?!"

"No, Tommy, I didn't. I figured if I told them all about what the woman told me, our parents would never let us come back here and then I wouldn't be able to help her."

Tommy and Meagen both glared at Rinnah with looks that told her she knew better.

"Yeah, I know, not original programming. But I guess I kinda feel responsible, you know? Like I have to help her now."

Rinnah glanced to the front seat to see if the adults were still preoccupied.

"I'll not have the children eating cardboard for dinner," Mrs. Lane was saying. She then shook her head and eyed the grocery list. "Frozen pizza. The very idea!"

As Mr. Paige backpedaled, Meagen brought Rinnah's attention back to the stranger at the fish hatchery.

"So what did she say to you?" she whispered. "Did she say someone was chasing her? Why? Why was someone chasing her?"

"Easy, Meagen. I don't have all the answers yet. But

here's what happened." Rinnah then launched into a detailed description of her encounter with the woman, culminating in a replay of the last words the woman spoke.

"'They're after the rose?'" Tommy repeated. "What does that mean?"

"I don't know. Yet. But it's a good thing we're staying in the Canyon. I have a feeling that any answers we find are going to be found here."

Rinnah pulled open the drawstrings of her bag and began to rummage through it.

"And there's something else. She gave me something before running away..."

Tommy and Meagen exchanged disbelieving glances.

"She gave you something? What?" Tommy asked and began to dig in Rinnah's bag as well. She slapped his hand away before removing the envelope and showing it to her friends, taking great care not to be seen from the grown-ups in the front seat.

"A letter?" Meagen asked.

Rinnah carefully opened the envelope and removed the note. With a quick glance up front to make sure she wasn't being watched, she opened the note and held it in her lap as Tommy and Meagen read.

"Uh, hello?" Meagen said when she was done. "As if *that* makes any sense!"

Upon hearing Meagen, Mrs. Lane thrust her large face from around the headrest.

"Hmmm?"

With the woman peering over her glasses, Meagen blushed and squirmed uncomfortably in her seat. Rinnah, startled at Mrs. Lane's sudden curiosity, had shoved the note safely back into her bag. It was nowhere in sight, although she caught Mrs. Lane searching the back seat with her eyes.

"Oh, uh … nothing. I just saw a, uh, dead dog on the side of the highway."

Mrs. Lane frowned.

"Poor creature must have jumped from the back of a truck."

At that, she turned back around in her seat and soon the sound of a paper grocery bag being shuffled about could be heard.

"Loud, much?" Rinnah whispered.

"Sorry," Meagen mouthed.

Tommy leaned forward, watching the back of Mrs. Lane's bobbing head, and spoke from the side of his mouth in an effort to not be overheard.

"What do you think it means?"

Rinnah bit her bottom lip and thought for a moment.

"Well, I dunno," she began. "I think we should do some

research on 'the Rose' and find out what that means, if anything."

Meagen, eager to make up for her backseat blunder, hurried in with her own ideas.

"I brought my laptop. We can search the Internet as soon as we get to the cabin."

"Do what when we get to the cabin?" a voice from the front seat asked.

The kids jumped as Mrs. Lane once again peered at them from the front seat. They couldn't look guiltier of something if they tried.

"Hmmm?"

Mrs. Lane, holding a pink box of bakery brownies, eyed the kids suspiciously. Rinnah glanced at the rearview mirror, and saw Mr. Paige shift his gaze from the road to the mirror, and then back again. His eyes held no curiosity when they met hers, making Rinnah think that he wasn't very interested in what was going on in the back seat.

Rinnah glanced back at Mrs. Lane and saw a look of warning pass over the woman's features. She fidgeted in her seat. How much had she heard?

"Oh, you know. Plan stuff to do tomorrow and junk."

Mrs. Lane looked doubtful.

"Well, you kids can have this as a snack until I can get a proper dinner inside you." She thrust the box further into the back seat, which Tommy eagerly accepted. After taking an especially large one, he passed the brownies to the girls. Rinnah took one and caught a lingering gaze from Mrs. Lane. She bit into the brownie and flashed a chocolate-covered grin. With a cluck, Mrs. Lane returned to rummaging through a paper bag that sat somewhere on the floorboard.

The sun was setting as the Jeep followed the unpaved road back from the main highway. Rounding a group of evergreen trees, a beautiful cedar-shingled cabin came into view. The chimney attached to the side of the picturesque cottage was made of river rock and covered in the wild vines of a climbing rose bush, the yellow roses tossing petals with each breeze. A deep porch sat in front, with more rose bushes lining the wide stoop. Huge lilac bushes lined the edges of the property, and fat, fragrant blooms hung from the branches like great bunches of lavender grapes.

"Wow!" Rinnah said as she slammed the door shut. "This place is awesome!"

Meagen agreed with a squeal of delight and made a run for the front door.

"It's like a dream..." Mrs. Lane said as she pulled grocery bags from the back of the Jeep. Tommy acted unimpressed as he untied the rope that secured suitcases to the top of the Jeep, but Rinnah could tell he was just as captivated with the cabin as the rest of them. Mr. Paige and Mrs. Lane unloaded several boxes of groceries and followed the kids into the house.

Once inside, Mrs. Lane and the kids marveled at how large the cabin actually was. Mr. Paige took them on a brief tour, immediately showing Rinnah and Meagen the bedroom they would be sharing. Then they were shown Mrs. Lane's room, conveniently located just off the country-style kitchen. Mr. Paige was especially proud of his room, the master bedroom with its own bathroom and an entire wall made out of sliding glass doors that opened onto a deck. The group stood out on the deck as the sun set, enjoying the sounds of the local wildlife and a brook that bubbled just below. Rinnah soon noticed that Tommy had grown unusually quiet.

"What's up?" she asked as the group made its way back into the living room. Mr. Paige had stacked kindling in the fireplace and was just lighting it when he heard the kids enter.

"All the bedrooms are taken. Which means *I* have to sleep on some lumpy sofa."

Mr. Paige closed the screen on the fireplace and stood. Rinnah noticed that he was grinning as he wiped soot onto his jeans.

"No, Tommy. You won't have to sleep on 'some lumpy sofa.' In fact, I think you've got the best room in the whole place!"

"I do?"

"Just follow me."

Mr. Paige walked away from the fireplace and rounded the corner. Tommy shrugged and followed, with the girls close behind.

Set back from the edge of the fireplace was a doorway that Rinnah had mistook for another way into the kitchen. There, Mr. Paige had paused and, seeing the kids looking expectantly, pointed up toward the cathedral ceilings. Tommy followed the roofline with his eyes until he saw something that made him jump in surprise.

"Score!"

Just above them, a small loft overlooked the living room.

Tommy pushed past Mr. Paige and soon his footfalls could be heard bounding up the tucked-away staircase. Momentarily, Tommy appeared at the railing and waved down at the girls.

"That takes care of that," Mr. Paige said and went back to the fire to add a large log to the now-crackling kindling.

Rinnah and Meagen elbowed each other through the doorway and up the stairs. They scrambled into the loft space to find a twin bed made out of oak with a matching nightstand. The space was built into the nook created by the steep pitch of the roof as it met the back wall of the house. Positioned against the back wall, the bed couldn't be seen from the downstairs area. In fact, one would have to bend over to crawl into bed, the ceiling was so low. But at the railing, the kids could stand at full height and survey most of the living area. Mr. Paige was stoking the fire as Mrs. Lane emerged from the kitchen, wiping her hands on a dishtowel.

"Hey! Let's spit and see if we can hit the couch from here!"

Upon hearing Tommy's alarming suggestion, Mrs. Lane looked up with a start.

"My goodness! I didn't notice that when we got here," she remarked to Mr. Paige. She smiled and walked further into the living room. As she surveyed the loft space, she called up to the kids.

"Dinner will be ready in an hour. That should give you enough time to unpack and get settled in."

With that, Mrs. Lane turned and made for the kitchen.

"And keep your saliva in your mouth, Tommy," she called over her shoulder.

Meagen scrunched her face in disgust and backed away from Tommy.

"When you're done here, meet us back in our room so we can get on the Internet and start looking up stuff on the Rose," Rinnah said.

"We need to make sure there's a phone jack in there for the connection," Meagen added.

Just as she turned away from the railing, Rinnah froze.

Mrs. Lane's screams ripped through the cabin like the shriek of a siren.

HOORAY FOR HOLLYWOOD

CHAPTER SIX

"MRS. LANE!"

The kids flew down the stairs and ran into the kitchen, nearly colliding with Mr. Paige along the way.

"What's wrong?" Mr. Paige demanded.

Mrs. Lane, looking pale and shaking, pointed out the kitchen window.

"There's a man outside," she said in a terrified whisper. "It's the man who killed that poor woman at the fish hatchery, I just know it!"

As Mrs. Lane spoke, Meagen's dad moved slowly

toward the back door. When he got there, he switched on the porch light and opened the door.

"Hello?" he asked.

Rinnah watched as a figure shifted in the shadows. When a man moved into the circle of light cast from the porch lamp, Rinnah made a quick inspection. First, she noticed how handsome he was. Like, movie star handsome. She felt a girlish nudge from Meagen, but didn't take her eyes off the guy on the porch. Rinnah judged him to be about 25 years old. She watched as he ran a large, callused hand through the dark brown, wavy hair that spilled over his eyes. A small beard and mustache struggled to form a goatee over his otherwise smooth and tan features. He wore jeans and a wool plaid shirt over a gray T-shirt. Heavy and well-worn work boots covered his feet. Rinnah thought that, despite his good looks, he appeared quite unassuming—if indeed this man were responsible for the attack on the mysterious foreign woman.

Mrs. Lane stood rigid and appeared as if she would knock him a good one if he was to stir even in the slightest. The man looked around at Rinnah and her friends. He fidgeted from his place on the porch stoop and timidly began to speak.

"Bill Paige?" he asked. Meagen's dad nodded, but didn't yet invite the man in.

"I didn't mean to scare anyone," he said. No one spoke as all eyes remained locked on the young man in the doorway. He blushed and looked behind him, seeming to not know if he should just leave or not.

"Can I help you?" Mr. Paige asked when the man offered nothing more.

"Oh, sorry," he said. "I'm Ben Forrest. I brought the spare set of keys."

Mr. Paige sighed with a hint of embarrassment and opened the door wider for Ben to come into the kitchen.

"I noticed the lights on in the house and came to the back door to take a look." Then, with a look of confusion, "You weren't expected until tomorrow. I thought someone might be robbing the place..."

Mr. Paige offered Ben a friendly handshake. He accepted and allowed himself to be led into the kitchen.

"Everyone," Mr. Paige said, "I would like you all to meet our landlord." Then, with an embarrassed glance to Ben, "He owns this cabin."

Mrs. Lane sighed heavily and clutched a dishtowel to her chest.

"Good heavens! You've given me such a fright." Then she hurried forward and took Ben's hand. "I'm Mrs. Lane, a friend of the family's."

Ben offered her a sheepish grin.

"I'm sorry I frightened you."

Mrs. Lane silently chided herself as Mr. Paige introduced the kids.

"He's gorgeous!" Meagen whispered in Rinnah's ear. Tommy heard her and rolled his eyes. Ben heard her too. He laughed, displaying a sparkling, heart-skipping smile. Rinnah thought Meagen would faint from the sight of it.

"I'm so sorry, Ben," Mr. Paige said when the introductions were finished. "I wanted to get an early start in the morning on my project. I was in such a hurry, I guess I forgot to call."

"That's okay," he said. "I'm just glad to finally meet all of you."

Mrs. Lane busied herself with light kitchen duties as the rest of the group took seats at the kitchen table. Tommy shot Ben an exaggerated look of suspicion. He began to question his new landlord like a detective in an old movie.

"So where were *you* when someone tried to kill that woman at the fish hatchery?"

Mrs. Lane gasped and dropped a handful of silverware.

"Don't mind him," Meagen said with glare in Tommy's direction. "He's a little hard-of-thinking."

Tommy frowned, but waited for Ben to answer. Rinnah did too.

"That's all right," Ben said. "I guess I don't mind the question. It's not the first time I was asked that today."

Rinnah stopped breathing and looked at Ben. He blushed under her stare and let his blue-eyed gaze drop to the kitchen table. He looked as if he said too much and regretted it.

"Oh?" Rinnah said. She felt a tingle and tugged at the medicine bag that swung from her neck. She had forgotten she still had it on, and tossed it over her shoulder.

"That was at 3:30 this afternoon, from what I've been told," Ben explained. He picked at a piece of Formica that had come loose from the edge of the table. Rinnah gave Tommy a curious glance. He responded with a quick nod and a serious expression.

"About that time, I was home doing some paperwork. And before you ask, the answer's no. No one saw me there."

So he has no alibi, Rinnah thought to herself. And not only that, someone else had asked him the same thing. The police? Rinnah made a note of the possibility. Without a connection to the foreigner, it meant absolutely zilch. She decided to find out more about this Mr. Ben Forrest.

"Enough of that," Mr. Paige said. "It's none of our business, anyway." He gave Rinnah and Tommy a behave-yourself look and stood from the table. Ben followed and made as if to leave.

"No, no, no! You sit right back down," Mrs. Lane commanded. "At least let me apologize by having you to dinner."

Ben turned in his chair and followed the bustling Mrs. Lane with his eyes as she pinballed from one corner of the kitchen to the other.

"That's really not necessary. I—"

"It's not a question, Mr. Forrest," she interrupted. "Don't you move from that chair!"

Ben turned to Mr. Paige with a pleading look in his eyes. Meagen's father merely responded by raising his eyebrows, as if to say, "I dare you."

Half an hour later, the girls were in their room. They were busy unpacking their belongings and filling a chest of drawers with summer clothes. Rinnah sat on a squeaky bed and pulled open her backpack.

"So what's your take on Ben?" she asked, as she searched her bag for the mysterious note.

"Total hottie," Meagen said.

Rinnah frowned and stopped digging.

"That's not exactly what I meant."

Meagen jumped on the bed next to Rinnah, holding a toothbrush and grinning.

"I know what you meant. As soon as I heard that crack

about being asked twice for an alibi, I knew you would go all Teen Investigator."

Rinnah's brown, almond eyes flashed.

"Exactly!" she said. "For some reason, someone else had asked him the same question Tommy did. Why?"

Meagen shrugged and tapped her toothbrush against her chin.

"Maybe he's had some kind of run-in with the cops in the past," she suggested.

Rinnah nodded enthusiastically. "That's what I'm thinking."

She returned to her backpack and held it open to better see inside.

"I wonder how I can find out for sure?" she thought aloud as she finally found the note. One of Rinnah's pink plastic hair clips with a row of tiny rosebuds was hanging onto a corner of the envelope. She pulled the note free and tossed the clip back into her bag.

Meagen watched as her friend shoved the note into the front pocket of her jeans. She frowned and shook her head.

"I think you need to be careful, Rinnah," Meagen said. "Remember what happened last summer—you nearly got in over your pigtails."

Rinnah rolled her eyes and stood to leave.

"Everything turned out fine. Besides," she said as she grasped Meagen's hand and pulled her from the bed. "I'm sure you're just dying to know more about Hunky Ben."

Meagen giggled and produced a tube of lip gloss from her dresser drawer. She applied it while looking into a mirror draped with a pink scarf.

As they made to leave the room, Rinnah froze and looked over Meagen's head.

"What's up?" Meagen asked. She stood from the bed and looked behind her.

A cold breeze came in from the open window above the bed, causing Rinnah's hair to ruffle.

"I thought I saw something..." Rinnah said. She crawled across the bed and leaned out the open window. Peering into the darkness, Rinnah could just make out the vague outlines of evergreen trees shifting in the wind. Shadows danced across the face of a steep cliff just beyond the woods, and the sound of a babbling creek gurgled in her ears. Meagen joined her at the windowsill and looked around.

"I don't see anything. Must've been the trees."

Just then, a loud splash interrupted the calm sounds of the creek, causing Rinnah and Meagen to jump.

"How far are we from the main highway?" Rinnah asked.

"About a mile."

Rinnah continued staring into the woods.

"Are there any other cabins out here?"

Meagen sat back, away from the open window, before answering.

"The closest ones are on the other side of the highway, I think."

Rinnah turned and gazed at her friend. She found goosebumps rising on the backs of her arms and rubbed them down with the palms of her hands. The medicine bag bounced across her chest as she did so. Finally, she turned back and closed the window. Suddenly, the remoteness of the cabin didn't feel as good as it did when she arrived.

"Remind me not to be alone here after dark."

AN INTERESTING DINNER

CHAPTER SEVEN

AS THE GIRLS made their way to the dining room, they found Tommy sprawled on the sofa in front of the TV. He frowned as he tried to unhook three large, metal rings from each other.

"Watcha doin', Tom?" Meagen asked. She lingered beside the sofa and gazed at the console television set. Rinnah stood beside her and noticed an old-fashioned rabbit-ear antenna protruding from the box.

"Practicing my magic act," he said with disgust. "Or trying to." Then he noticed the girls watching TV.

"I guess they never heard of cable out here. The news is the only thing that antique can pick up."

Indeed, the local news station came in reasonably clear. Just as Rinnah began to turn toward the dining room, something she saw on the TV screen made her stop.

"Ooh! Turn it up," she said.

As Tommy got up and walked to the TV, mumbling something about the lack of a remote, Rinnah took a seat next to Meagen on the sofa.

The kids watched as a young news reporter with handsome, award-winning looks spoke into a microphone. Just over his head loomed a sign that read, "D.C. Booth Historic Fish Hatchery."

"That's where we were today, yeah?" Tommy said as he joined his friends on the sofa. Rinnah shushed him and hunched forward in an effort to hear the report.

"The Wild West Days took a deadly turn today when an unknown woman became the victim of attempted murder in this fish hatchery," the reporter said. He walked over to the pond from which the woman was pulled and gestured dramatically. "It was here that the woman was found floating this afternoon."

A group of obnoxious teenagers walked into the frame behind the reporter and made faces to the camera. Meagen clucked disapprovingly and continued watching.

"The woman was rushed to Spearfish General Hospital and remains in critical condition."

Someone off-camera must have said something to the teenagers, for they made obscene hand gestures and walked away.

"Police are searching for any possible clues as to the woman's identity. They have asked the public to come forward with any information that could help in their ongoing investigation. This is Travis Ruff, reporting live from Spearfish Canyon."

Back in the studio, a pretty blond woman continued the report by saying, "If you have any information about this case, please call 1-800-555-HELP. You can also log on to www.ActionNews-Canyon.com for more information on any of our top stories."

Just then, Mrs. Lane yelled from the kitchen.

"Dinner's ready!"

The kids didn't move. Rinnah knew what was coming from her friends and prepared herself for it.

"Did ya hear that, Rinnah?" Tommy asked.

"Yes, Tommy. Dinner's ready."

Tommy frowned. "Not that. The police—they're look-ing for people who know something about that lady in the fish pond."

Meagen nodded in agreement.

"Tom's right, Rinnah. You should call the police and tell them you talked to her. And show them that note!"

Rinnah fell back into the sofa and crossed her arms with a scowl.

"I will," she said. "Just as soon as I find out more about this 'Rose' thing."

Tommy grunted in exasperation and shook his head. Rinnah could tell by the look Meagen was giving her that she was not satisfied in the least with Rinnah's plan of action.

The kids sat in silence, each one thinking of the best way to handle the situation. Their eyes lingered on the TV screen, where the blonde's partner was delivering another story.

"...announced last week. Dakota High School Senior, Katharine Black Elk, had this to say about her election as this year's Spearfish Princess."

The report cut to a taped interview with Katharine, a very pretty girl with long black hair and sparkling brown eyes. Rinnah recognized the Trading Post Gift Shop at Rosebud that the girl and her interviewer stood in front of.

"Wow! Katharine's on TV!" Tommy cried when he saw the girl's face appear on the screen. "Old Ronnie must be calling every phone number on the rez."

Rinnah giggled and remembered that he had called

everyone, including her mom, last month when her selection was announced.

"Old Ronnie?" Meagen asked.

"Ronnie Black Elk," Rinnah answered. "Her grandfather. He's the medicine man for our tribe."

"There he is!" Tommy said with a finger pointed at the TV.

Nearly out of frame stood an older Indian man beaming proudly at his granddaughter.

Then Rinnah felt a stirring of curiosity as she held the medicine bag, the one that Ronnie had blessed. The one with the rose petals. Did he know something about the Rose? Rinnah thought about this as she watched Katharine on TV.

"I'm extremely happy to be chosen as this year's Indian representative," the girl said, "particularly because of my desire to preserve the culture indigenous to this part of the country. The Indian people have a lot to offer, not only in the arts, but to the local economy."

The report cut back to the studio, where the newscaster continued by saying, "You can meet Miss Black Elk tomorrow at Spearfish Community Park, where she will be speaking at the Sioux Memorial dedication ceremony."

Suddenly, the screen went black and Rinnah looked up

to see Mrs. Lane standing next to the TV. Her finger was still on the power button.

"Our landlord is here, remember?" she said with a look of disapproval. As Rinnah was about to stand, a knock came at the front door.

"Now what?" Mrs. Lane wiped her hands on a dish-towel and went to answer the door. "Well, hello! What a wonderful surprise!"

Mrs. Lane opened the door wider, and in walked Sandy Price. She was dressed casually in pressed jeans and a crisp, white linen blouse. She suddenly seemed unsure of herself and looked around the room self-consciously.

"I'm sorry. I thought I was expected."

"You are," Mr. Paige said as he entered from the kitchen. The look of uncertainty melted from Sandy's eyes and flashed to a twinkle when Meagen's father stepped forward and gave her a kiss on the cheek. Rinnah caught her breath and looked at Meagen. She found her friend frozen halfway up from the sofa, looking startled.

"Oops," Rinnah whispered. She watched as the look on Meagen's face took on a harder edge. Understanding colored her friend's face like a veil of scarlet lace.

She's getting it now, Rinnah thought to herself. She heard Mr. Paige speaking and tore her eyes away from Meagen.

"With all the excitement," Meagen's dad was explaining, "I forgot to mention that Sandy would be joining us."

Mrs. Lane beamed at the woman and said, "Good! I tend to cook way too much food. I hope you're hungry."

"Starving," Sandy nodded, looking much more at ease than she did a few moments ago.

Mr. Paige ushered Sandy into the living room.

"Kids," he said. "We have another guest for dinner."

Tommy bounded forward and offered Sandy a gentlemanly handshake. Meagen, however, sat back down.

"Hey, Sandy," Rinnah said. She stood and waved, but wasn't yet ready to leave Meagen.

Sandy smiled and looked from Rinnah to Meagen sitting sullen on the sofa. The silence lingered, and Rinnah found herself feeling uncomfortable. She slipped her hands into the back pockets of her jeans and swayed on the balls of her feet. She finally just shrugged.

"Meagen," Mr. Paige said with a scowl. "Sandy's here for dinner. Want to say 'Hi'?"

Meagen stood with an exaggerated smile.

"Hey, Sandy."

Sandy offered Meagen a nervous smile, her gaze going from the girl to her father, and then back again.

"Hey, Meagen," she offered. "How do you like the cabin? I helped your father find it."

Meagen smiled even wider, showing every single one of her bright, shiny teeth. Rinnah threw an arm around Meagen and gave her a subtle buddy-hug warning. Meagen finally answered when Rinnah gave her a little hip check.

"It's great. Nice and out-of-the-way like."

Mr. Paige frowned briefly at his daughter. He then gestured toward the kitchen.

"Well, I think Mrs. Lane has outdone herself for her first night. What'dya say we get some grub?"

Mr. Paige led Sandy toward the dining room, tossing Meagen a behave-yourself glance over his shoulder.

" 'I helped your father find it.' " Meagen mocked when the two were out of earshot. Rinnah gave her friend's shoulder a quick squeeze.

"Chill, Meagen. It's just dinner, OK?"

Meagen frowned, but didn't move. Rinnah thought a moment and then walked away.

"I wonder how Ben's doing?" she asked with a careless look over her shoulder. Meagen's eyebrows flew up at the mention of their new landlord. She hesitated briefly before nodding her head and skipping toward the dining room.

Ben was already seated at a fully set table, but stood when Mr. Paige introduced Sandy. The two shook hands before Meagen's dad slid out a chair and offered it to Sandy. He then took a seat next to her and gave Sandy's hand a little squeeze before grabbing a napkin.

Meagen made a beeline for the empty chair next to Ben. It wasn't lost on Tommy, who threw Rinnah a questioning glance before plopping into a chair at the end of the table.

"Would you like some iced tea, Mr. Forrest?" Mrs. Lane asked.

"Please, call me Ben. And yes, I would like some very much, thanks." He offered Mrs. Lane a thousand-watt smile, causing her to titter girlishly. Just as Mrs. Lane turned to leave, Meagen jumped up from her seat.

"I'll get it!"

As she got to the kitchen doorway, Meagen turned and smiled at Ben.

"Oh, gross!" Tommy said as he reached for the mountain of mashed potatoes stuffed into an antique mixing bowl. Rinnah raised an eyebrow when Meagen came back into the dining room carrying a pitcher of iced tea.

While a platter of roast beef made its way around the table, Rinnah started the conversation.

"So which construction company do you work for, Mr. Forrest?"

Ben scooped green beans from a dish and looked up.

"How'd you know I worked in construction?"

"Your boots," Rinnah replied. "They're standard issue."

Ben smiled and passed the green beans to Meagen.

"And your strong hands," Meagen said when she retrieved the beans.

Mr. Paige furrowed his brow, and Tommy rolled his eyes. Meagen caught both and was immediately silenced.

"I'm working on the new Chamber of Commerce project with the Little Horn crew."

Tommy laughed, his mouth wide open and displaying a disgusting mush of mashed potatoes and roast beef.

"Ew!" Rinnah said as she knocked him one with her elbow.

"What's so funny?" Ben asked, looking around the table in confusion.

"It's just that we know the Little Horns," explained Rinnah. "We went to school with Victor."

"Aaah," Ben nodded as he ladled gravy onto his potatoes. "He can be a little … difficult. To get to know, I mean."

"You could say that," Rinnah answered.

"He's a loser," Tommy said.

Mr. Paige looked at Tommy and cleared his throat. "Well, Tommy. He's just got a different life than we have, that's all."

Tommy shoveled some green beans into his mouth and gave a muffled, "Uh huh."

Sensing a sore subject, Sandy chimed in to change it.

"So, do you own this place, Ben?" she asked. Ben held up his finger while nodding his head and chewing. Finally, he answered.

"Yes. It belonged to my grandparents who retired here from Los Angeles. They left it to me, and now I take care of the place."

"How come you don't live here?" Rinnah asked.

"Too big, I guess. I like my little one bedroom cabin further down the highway. Plus, the income from renting it out really comes in handy."

Rinnah finished chewing some bread and swallowed, allowing questions to form in her mind. She chose one and asked it.

"Are you from here?"

Ben shook his head.

"No. I grew up in Los Angeles. Didn't like it. At all. So when my grandparents left me their house, I moved out here." He took a drink of his iced tea and continued. "My folks still live in L.A., but I don't get out there much."

Tommy took up the conversation then.

"There's a director named Forrest I really like. He does all those action movies, yeah? Like *Too Young to Die*. Did you see that one?"

Ben smiled. "Sure did. And the sequel, *Still Too Young to Die*."

Tommy looked at the ceiling thinking. "What was his name? Frank Forrest?"

"Hank." Ben corrected.

"Yeah. That's it!" Tommy said. "Hank Forrest. His movies are so cool!"

"Did you ever meet any movie stars when you lived in L.A.?" Meagen asked, finally finding the courage to enter the conversation. She kept here eyes away from Sandy.

"Oh, a few, I guess."

Meagen squealed and nearly spilled her glass of tea when her hands flew to her face. "Omigod! Who? Who have you seen?"

Ben began to laugh and something suddenly dawned on Rinnah.

"He's your dad!"

"Huh?" Ben looked up, still grinning.

"Hank Forrest. He's your dad, isn't he?" Rinnah asked.

Tommy and Meagen both gasped and stared openly at Ben. Smiling even still, he turned to Mr. Paige and said, "There's no secrets with this one, is there?"

Mr. Paige scooped more potatoes from the bowl. "Nope."

"NO WAY!" cried Tommy. "Hank Forrest is your *dad?*"

Ben laughed outright. "I'm in for it now!"

Rinnah saw that Ben was beaming, obviously very proud of his father. Why, then, was he living way out in the middle of South Dakota? What happened back in L.A. to make him hate it so much?

One thing's for sure, Rinnah thought. *I'm gonna find out if it's the last thing I do.*

A CLUE REVEALED

CHAPTER EIGHT

RINNAH SAT AT the breakfast table chewing toast and drinking orange juice. Early morning sunlight poured in through the kitchen window and spilled over a vase filled with beautiful, fragrant roses and lilacs. Rinnah gazed at the flowers that sat before her and silently scolded herself for passing out on the sofa right after dinner the night before. She didn't even remember getting into bed. What she did remember was that Sandy had seemed like a very nice lady. And Ben ... well, he was an interesting mystery. She wished she had stayed awake and at least talked to him a bit more before he left. Plus, she didn't get a chance to search the Internet for any information on the Rose.

"It's a glorious Sunday morning," Mrs. Lane trilled. "The first day of July—it has to be my favorite month. Makes me think of watermelon and skinny-dip—"

She suddenly fell silent and blushed, although a smile tugged at the corners of her mouth. Meagen giggled in delight, while Tommy simply looked terrified.

"Anyhoo," she continued. "What are you kids up to today?"

Meagen pored over the morning edition of the *Spearfish Sentinel*, while Tommy read a book titled *101 Feats of Illusion: The Beginner's Edition*.

"What *aren't* we going to do?" Meagen said as she folded the paper to the "Activities" section. "The Belle Fourche rodeo started yesterday, there's a barbecue at the park in Spearfish, the Sioux Memorial dedication, and tons of stuff going on right through the week. I can't wait for the big parade on July 4th."

"Ooooh! A parade!" Mrs. Lane squealed.

Rinnah noticed the humorous look in Mr. Paige's eyes as he stood to get more coffee.

"Yep!" explained Tommy. "It's the big Independence Day kick-off!"

Suddenly Rinnah froze.

"Independence," she mumbled. Bells were going off in her head. And fireworks. "July 4th. Independence Day."

Rinnah leapt from the table and ran from the room. Tommy and Meagen exchanged a quick look before jumping up and following. Mrs. Lane just shook her head and put the carton of orange juice into the refrigerator.

Back in her room, Rinnah was on her knees frantically searching through a pile of yesterday's dirty laundry when Tommy and Meagen burst in.

"What's up?" Tommy asked. Rinnah found what she was looking for and stood. She held the shorts she wore yesterday and searched the pockets.

"I think I may have figured it out," she said in a breathless whisper.

Tommy and Meagen moved in close.

"The note!" Rinnah said as she realized she had stuffed it into her bag. "I think I know what some of it means."

Meagen gasped as Rinnah grabbed the note from her bag, pulled the parchment from the envelope, and read it aloud.

Lily –
The time has come for our independence. Take great care under their stony gaze, for the exploding heavens shall illuminate our deeds.

They've sent the Florist -- they know we are here and are after the Rose.

   - Sage

"The time has come for our independence," she repeated.

Rinnah looked up at Tommy and Meagen, but was met with blank stares. She sighed in exasperation and waved the note in front of their faces.

"Independence," she said.

Tommy looked at Meagen and shrugged.

"Independence *Day*," she explained. "July 4th."

Suddenly, Rinnah could practically see the light bulb go on above Meagen's head.

"Yeah!" she cried. "Something's gonna happen on July 4th. That's Wednesday!"

Rinnah went back to the note.

"The exploding heavens shall illuminate our deeds." Rinnah looked up.

"Fireworks!" Tommy guessed.

Meagen reached up and gingerly took the note from Rinnah's hand.

"The note is signed by someone named Sage. How will we ever find out who that is?"

Rinnah read the note again from Meagen's side and said, "The 'Florist.'"

"Huh?"

" 'They've sent the Florist.' "

Tommy and Meagen stood thinking while Rinnah continued examining the note.

"And I'll bet that 'Lily' is the lady who gave me this message. The one someone tried to kill."

Tommy and Meagen looked on in silence as Rinnah continued thinking aloud.

"She was way scared when she gave me this note. I think it was a message that only she was meant to get. But she gave it to me ... thinking I could somehow help."

"Why did she think *you* could help?" Tommy asked.

Rinnah shook her head. "That's what I would like to know. But I think one thing's for sure. I think she saw someone at the Wild West Days. Someone that scared her bad enough to ditch this message."

"Someone who shouldn't know about this note."

Rinnah looked up and agreed with Meagen by nodding her head.

Rinnah shivered and shoved the note back into its envelope. Then she put it into her backpack.

"I think the first thing we should do today is check out your dad's new office, Meagen."

Meagen seemed confused. "Why's that?"

Tommy spoke up, realizing that not only did Rinnah

have a plan, but that he knew what it was. Which didn't seem to happen too often.

"That lady is at the hospital, yeah? You wanna see if she's gotten better, and maybe talk to her some more."

"Right, Tommy," Rinnah answered. "Let's go ask Mr. Paige for a ride."

As Tommy and Meagen made their way from the room, Rinnah spotted the medicine bag her grandmother gave her dangling from a bedside lamp. She wondered if it would really work as protection from any unknown dangers. She shrugged and snatched it free. Stopping before the dressing table mirror, she put it around her neck before joining her friends in the living room. When she got there, Meagen was already talking to her dad about going to the hospital.

"So, we wanted to see where you work, and then hang out downtown for a while."

Meagen was following her father as he searched for his briefcase.

"That's fine, hon. But I'm going to be very busy. Sunday is the only day they would let me take the billing systems offline. And they only gave me two hours to do it. I can't show you around as much as I would like."

"That's OK. We just want to see where you work. This is the first time you've worked with a hospital, isn't it?"

"Yep," her dad replied. He found his briefcase next to the living room sofa. He checked his watch and sighed.

"We better get a move on, or I'm going to be late." With that, the kids scurried around grabbing backpacks and light jackets before following Mr. Paige out the front door.

The day was absolutely gorgeous and smelled wonderful from all the roses and lilacs in full bloom. The sounds of the brook behind the house could be heard, as well as all sorts of Canyon wildlife.

"When we get back from the hospital," Rinnah whispered on the way to the Jeep, "let's get online and do a name search for Ben and his dad. With a famous father, were bound to find something on your new boyfriend."

Meagen ignored the "boyfriend" remark and jumped into the front seat. Rinnah settled into the back seat with Tommy and began to think.

If the police questioned Ben, then there must be a reason, she thought to herself. *And he has no alibi for the time when the woman was attacked.*

But Rinnah didn't think the two were connected. She didn't know Ben that well, but he didn't strike her as someone who would attack a woman in broad daylight. That would be the work of someone desperate. And Ben didn't seem the desperate type. Or the murderous type.

Without realizing it, Rinnah clasped the medicine bag

tightly in her hand as another thought sprung from the depths of her mind.

The killer hadn't completed the job. He risked getting caught by attacking in public. That showed a level of desperation that bordered on insanity.

Rinnah was sure of one thing—the same thought she was having now, was also one the killer was having. About that poor woman at the fish hatchery. The one who seemed so scared.

She wasn't dead yet.

DANGER AT SPEARFISH GENERAL

CHAPTER NINE

RINNAH FOUND HERSELF gazing out the Jeep's window, watching the evergreen trees of the Black Hills Forest speed past her in a green-and-brown blur. Tommy and Meagen were as silent as Rinnah. Suddenly, Mr. Paige honked the horn in three short blasts, causing Rinnah to scan the roadside.

Mr. Paige slowed as he went around a curve and waved his hand from the window. Looking across the highway, Rinnah could see a small, A-frame cabin. Getting out of a pick-up truck was Ben Forrest. Upon hearing the horn, he turned and recognized the Jeep and its passengers. He offered a smile and a friendly wave.

Just as the Jeep pulled out of the curve, Rinnah spotted someone else coming out of truck. The young man walked to the tailgate and removed a toolbox from the bed. His long hair and swagger was immediately familiar. It was Victor Little Horn.

"Oh, great!" Tommy groaned from Rinnah's side. Meagen frowned and questioned Rinnah with a glance from the front seat. Rinnah merely shrugged and looked back at the cabin. Victor's gaze lingered on the Jeep until the cabin disappeared behind a grove of trees.

Rinnah sat back in her seat and felt the Jeep pick up speed as it came out of the curve. She furrowed her brow and wondered what those two could possibly find in common. Working together was one thing, but to hang out on a Sunday?

"Hmmm…"

Twenty minutes later, the Jeep pulled into the parking lot of Spearfish General Hospital.

"Oh my gosh!"

The gasp came from Meagen, causing Rinnah to rouse herself from her own thoughts. She looked up to see what Meagen found so interesting.

News vans with satellite dishes sprouting from their tops obscured the main entrance to the hospital. Dozens of reporters and cameramen milled about, drinking coffee from Styrofoam cups and speaking into cell phones and walkie-talkies.

"This place is a zoo!" Mr. Paige exclaimed.

Rinnah agreed, and suddenly couldn't get out of the Jeep fast enough. She was opening the door as the Jeep rolled to a stop in one of the few parking spots left.

"Hold it, guys!" Mr. Paige ordered.

Rinnah looked around and saw that Tommy and Meagen also had their doors open.

"Stay close to me," he continued as he shut off the ignition. "We're gonna have to go in the back way."

Finally, they all jumped out of the Jeep and followed Mr. Paige as he led them to the side of the hospital. They stopped before an unmarked door that required a key-pass entry. Mr. Paige pulled his wallet from a back pocket and removed a white plastic card with a magnetic strip. He inserted the card and a tiny red light went from red to green. The door unlocked with a metallic click, and Mr. Paige swung it open.

Moments later, they were walking down a brightly lit hallway with stainless steel gurneys against the far wall. At the intersection up ahead, Rinnah could make out a commotion in the main hall. A policeman was escorting a group of reporters back toward the main entrance, and frazzled nurses walked briskly between their station and other offices. A few patients in hospital gowns were trying to get the attention of nurses who politely told them to return to their rooms.

"What a mess!" Tommy observed.

Mr. Paige sighed and rubbed his forehead. His eyes lit up when he saw Sandy Price looking exasperated and speaking to a man in a rumpled suit. A uniformed police officer stood by and scribbled in a small note pad.

Sandy removed a pair of glasses from her white lab coat and put them on. Trying to ignore the chaos around her, she began flipping through multi-colored pages attached to a clear, plastic clipboard. Watching her read, Rinnah sensed an air of elegance, even in the lab coat. She studied the woman's impeccable posture and knew immediately that Sandy was in charge—despite the chaotic buzz around her.

"Sandy!" Mr. Paige called out.

Meagen rolled her eyes and slouched against the wall. "Great!"

Sandy turned and a look of recognition flickered across her face when her eyes fell on Mr. Paige. She waved off the man in the suit and walked down the hall toward Mr. Paige and the kids.

"I'm so sorry you have to deal with this on your first day," she said. "I'm right in the middle of a real mess. And I'm worried about what it will do to the hospital's reputation."

Mr. Paige looked behind her at the mass confusion in the main hallway.

"What's going on, anyway?" he said with a note of worry.

Sandy removed her glasses with trembling fingers.

"For one thing," she said, "the media has uncovered a story on the woman from the fish hatchery, and it's turned my hospital into a circus!"

Rinnah's ears pricked up at the mention of the mysterious woman and stepped forward.

"They found some kind of connection to European royalty," Sandy said with an exasperated wave of her hands. "She had a booth at the Wild West Days—some kind of mystical set-up, with crystals and fortune telling. A European version of the local, Native American spiritualism, the press is saying. They got her name from the application she filed for the booth. Her employees filled in the rest."

Sandy paused and didn't immediately continue with the story. Instead, her eyes stayed on Mr. Paige, and Rinnah sensed that she wasn't telling everything she knew. From the lingering gaze of Mr. Paige, Sandy's eyes glanced at Rinnah and her friends.

"There's more," she said when she returned her focus to Mr. Paige.

Suddenly, Sandy Price didn't look like the woman in control Rinnah saw just a moment ago. Away from the police, the media, and the general chaos they created, Sandy looked extremely vulnerable. Rinnah couldn't help but wonder what else was going on.

"It seems the guard posted at her door was called away and left without telling anyone..."

Rinnah felt her stomach flutter, and a sense of dread stifled the antiseptic hallway.

"When he returned to the room," Sandy continued, "he found the monitors unplugged, and..."

Mr. Paige sighed deeply and rubbed the back of his neck. Tommy and Meagen stood staring at the floor while Sandy fumbled with her glasses.

Finally, Rinnah broke the silence.

"She's dead?"

CAFFEINE, BOOKS, AND SOMEONE HIDING IN THE SHADOWS
CHAPTER TEN

AN HOUR LATER, the kids sat on an old sofa in Common Grounds, a funky coffeehouse on Main Street. As soon as Sandy Price told them about the death of the woman back at the hospital, Mr. Paige felt that the kids had better leave. So the gang left Meagen's dad to his first day on the job and walked several blocks in silence until they found a place where they could sit down and talk. After ordering sodas, and a café mocha for Meagen, the conversation began with talk of the Spearfish Police Department.

"But you have to tell them, Rinnah," Meagen pleaded.

"You may have seen the killer without even realizing it."

Rinnah fingered the straw in her Coke as she thought.

"That's what I'm wondering," she said. "I've played that scene in my mind like a hundred times since yesterday. I just didn't get a good enough look at that figure in the restroom doorway."

She closed her eyes and pored over the memory of the figure in the restroom doorway back at the fish hatchery. But try as she might, she just couldn't get any details beyond a vague shadow.

Meagen sighed and took a delicate slurp of her hot chocolate and coffee concoction. She thought about arguing further, but could tell by the look of determination in Rinnah's face that now would not be a good time to try reasoning with her. She decided to let the knowledge of the mysterious woman's death—murder, actually—cool off for a while.

"I can't believe that the killer got to her," Tommy said. "I mean, in the hospital of all places. With a guard and everything!"

Rinnah frowned at that. "You know, that's bugging me, too."

Meagen grimaced and shook off a chill.

"He did it with a pillow!" she whispered in disgust. "Just smothered her after disconnecting the monitors."

Rinnah nodded with a shiver of her own. "To be nice and quiet, probably."

Rinnah opened her backpack and pulled out a note pad. She read from it and looked up at the small bookstore in the loft space above the coffeehouse.

"Cassandra..."

"Huh?" Tommy questioned.

Rinnah focused her eyes back on her friends.

"That's her name. Cassandra," she answered. "I heard Sandy tell Meagen's dad." She paused and then offered, "No last name. Just 'Cassandra.'"

"Or Lily," Meagen said after she drained off the last of her café mocha.

"Yeah. Lily." Then she asked, "What country did Sandy say the woman came from?"

Meagen wiped her mouth on a napkin before answering. "Bulgaria."

"Oh, yeah," Tommy added. "She was some kinda radical or something."

"Right," Rinnah said as she dug out a pencil from her bag and began writing. "In some city I've never heard of. I think she called it 'Narnia' or something..."

Meagen shook her head and rolled her eyes.

"What?" Rinnah asked when she caught her friend's look.

"'Narnia' is from a book," Meagen explained. "As in *The Chronicles of*…"

Rinnah went back to scribbling. "Whatever."

Meagen furrowed her brow and looked at the ceiling as she tried to remember the name of the city Sandy said Lily came from. She remembered and snapped her fingers.

"Varna!"

Rinnah glanced up momentarily before adding the city's name to her notebook.

"V-a-r-n-a."

Then she waited for Meagen to check her spelling. When Meagen nodded, she underlined the word for emphasis.

"But what was she doing selling crystals at the Wild West Days?" Tommy asked.

Rinnah paused a minute before answering.

"Well, if you think about it," she said, chewing on her pencil, "it's kind of the perfect cover."

"Cover?" Tommy repeated.

"Yeah. Think about it. She doesn't look like she belongs here, you know? She's got this exotic-looking face, an accent, that kinda thing. She would stick out like a sore thumb. Unless…"

"Unless she totally plays it up," Meagen interrupted.

"Puts on a bright red scarf, wild jewelry, and sits in a booth selling crystals."

"Exactly!" Rinnah said.

Tommy looked puzzled. "But that still doesn't explain what she's under cover *from*."

Rinnah didn't have an answer for that one, and instead gazed at her friends thoughtfully until they all lapsed into their own quiet musings, each one oblivious to the comings and goings of the coffee house patrons around them. Rinnah began thinking of the drive over to Spearfish earlier that morning. She remembered seeing Victor get out of Ben's truck and realized it looked as if they were just pulling in. As she followed this train of thought, she gradually became aware of an odd tapping sound. She looked down and saw Meagen's tennis-shoed foot striking the leg of the coffee table that sat in front of the sofa.

Tap, tap, tap, tap.

Rinnah stared at her friend curiously. Finally, Meagen smiled and stood.

"You guys need another soda. I think I'll have another—"

"Uh," Rinnah interrupted. "I think you should just say no, girl."

"But—"

"Enough with the caffeine, already. You're bouncing off the walls!"

Meagen began to pout, but then Rinnah saw her eyes light up when the door to the coffeehouse opened.

"Tina!"

Tina Treadwell stopped in her tracks and looked momentarily startled. Then she smiled as Meagen skipped forward.

"What are YOU doing here?"

Tina looked around the coffeehouse before replying, "Oh. Well, I had to bring Mrs. Lane her car. And some clothes and things. You know. Thought I would grab an iced tea or something."

Tommy slurped loudly and waved at the young woman from his seat on the sofa.

"Tell us what's going on at the gallery," Rinnah said as she scooted over and made a place for Tina next to her on the couch.

Tina reluctantly sat down and offered a weaker grin than the one she wore just moments before. Rinnah watched as her eyes darted around the coffeehouse.

She's looking for someone, Rinnah thought. *I wonder if she has a secret boyfriend.* Rinnah grinned and looked around the room herself. As Meagen chattered on about spending the summer in the Canyon, Rinnah checked out the clientele.

In the two arm chairs at the other side of the coffee table sat a pair of elderly women enjoying what appeared to be hot tea and lemon poppyseed scones. Over at the tables in front of the street-side windows sat a small family of four lunching on sandwiches and cookies. Two old men played checkers at the game table, and a young girl cleared the table next to them.

Rinnah then looked at the order counter and saw a young man cleaning the Espresso machine.

Aha!

Rinnah's gaze lingered on the good-looking young man with ear piercings that matched Tina's. She giggled and turned to look at Tina.

Tina was listening to Meagen, but her eyes flickered between the girl and the upstairs bookstore.

Rinnah glanced up, still giggling, and looked back at the young man working the counter.

Then Rinnah froze.

She looked back up to the bookstore loft.

What was that?

The split-second memory of a person standing up at the second-floor railing flashed in her mind.

Rinnah peered farther into the bookstore that looked out over the coffeehouse and scanned the area.

The person was gone.

She looked harder at the book shelves and wire racks holding second-hand paperbacks.

Suddenly, a figure ducked behind a display of new fiction hardbacks.

Without thinking, Rinnah stood for a better look. Unfortunately, she couldn't see beyond the railing.

"Hm!" Rinnah cocked her head and stood on tiptoes, trying in vain to see past the railing. Then she gasped at something she saw between the slats of the railing.

"What's up?"

Rinnah jumped at the sound of Tommy's voice. When she turned back to Tina, she found the young woman looking quite startled, like she was just caught with her hand in the biscotti jar.

"Oh, I just see a new book I wanted to get," Rinnah offered lamely.

She sat back down then, but not before a quick glance to Tina confirmed her suspicions that whoever was up there was someone Tina knew. And by the way she nervously tugged at the silver pendant around her neck, she didn't want the kids to know.

Tina stood to leave, putting an end to the awkward silence that fell over the group.

"Well, guys," she said. "I should get that iced tea to go. I've got about a million things to do today and have to get back. That gallery can't run itself!"

While Tina placed her order with the pierced guy at the counter, Rinnah asked for a lift back to the cabin.

"Uh … sure. No problem."

Tommy and Meagen noticed her reluctance and exchanged glances.

Once Tina had her order, the kids followed her out of the shop and to Mrs. Lane's car.

No one spoke on the drive back to the cabin, except for the occasional tries from Meagen. But Tina only responded with absent "Mm Hmms," so Meagen finally gave up. Meanwhile, Rinnah sat and thought. Actually, she was remembering what she spotted between the slats of the railing back at Common Grounds. And it had her imagination working overtime.

Although the rest of his body was well hidden, his feet were not. As he stood hiding behind a rack of used books, Rinnah recognized the familiar work boots of Ben Forrest.

INTERNET INVESTIGATIONS

CHAPTER ELEVEN

"IT'S TIME WE LEARNED a little bit more about your boyfriend, Meagen."

The kids sat in the living room back at the cabin. Meagen had her laptop unpacked and was searching the room for a phone jack.

"Boyfriend?" Tommy asked. He glanced at Meagen, and Rinnah couldn't tell if he were only curious or perturbed.

"Ben Forrest," Rinnah replied. She scribbled notes into her tiny notebook until her pencil lead broke.

"Remind me to ask my mom for one of those Palm thingies."

"Rinnah, what are you talking about?"

Tommy looked completely baffled and his eyes darted between Rinnah and Meagen, searching their faces for clues.

"You know, those hand-held computers. I can keep notes, clues, times of death—"

"No, not that! *Ben!*"

"Oh," she replied casually. "He was at the coffee house."

Meagen gasped from behind the sofa. "He was there? Where?"

Rinnah threw the pencil down in disgust.

"Upstairs. In the bookstore."

Rinnah rummaged through her bag looking for another pencil to finish her notes.

"I definitely need to get on the Internet," she said, remembering to add Cassandra to her search, along with Ben Forrest and his father.

"But we didn't see him," Tommy said.

"There's probably a back stairway leading to the parking lot," Rinnah offered. "If he was there, that's how he got out."

"I wonder why the disappearing act," Tommy mused. Rinnah continued thinking out loud as Meagen studied baseboards.

"I don't think he wanted to be seen with Tina."

Meagen poked her head up from behind the table. "WHAT?!"

"He was there to see her," Rinnah explained. Then, off Meagen's blank stare, "Couldn't you tell she was there to meet someone?"

Tommy and Meagen remained mute, so Rinnah replayed Tina's visit back for them, adding her own take on the situation, like the way she behaved, her darting eyes, the look on her face when she realized Rinnah had seen Ben up in the book store. All the things that pointed to a secret meeting.

"Maybe they're, like, dating or something," Tommy offered when Rinnah was finished.

Rinnah thought a moment before replying, "Well, maybe. But why wouldn't they want anyone to know?" Tommy and Meagen had no answer for that. Finally, Meagen found a phone jack and an extra electrical outlet. After a few minutes, they made a makeshift desk with one of the two coffee tables.

"We can't stay on this too long," Meagen explained as she dialed in with the modem. "We're on the only phone line in the house."

After a few minutes of electrical pings and static, the browser page loaded and filled the screen. She quickly chose a search engine and looked to Rinnah.

"What do we look up first?"

Rinnah thought a moment. "Ben Forrest."

Meagen typed in the name and waited while the engine scoured the Internet for that name. Finally, a page was displayed. It showed 56 hits.

"I'll bet most of these are about his dad," Rinnah said and watched as Meagen clicked the first one.

"You're right," Meagen said. "This one is his bio on an entertainment Web site. It lists Ben as his son."

Meagen hit the back button and chose the next hit on the list. She did this six or seven times only to find more bios.

"How many entertainment sites are there, anyway?" Tommy asked. After looking at a couple more hits that lead to nothing informative, Meagen's hands flew from the keyboard.

"Der! How lame am I? I just remembered my dad has access to a periodical search engine." With that, she typed in www.e-pressarchives.com.

"This is a search engine for all kinds of news and magazine articles. It should bring up the kind of stuff we're looking for."

She typed in a password and was granted immediate access. She then typed in "Ben Forrest" in the search field and hit the SUBMIT button. After a few moments, the results page showed 18 hits in the form of newspaper and magazine headlines.

"Bingo!" Meagen said.

The kids huddled closer to the screen of the computer and scanned the headlines. Rinnah read what she saw aloud.

"'Director's Son Thumbs Nose at Tinseltown...,' 'Forrest Jr. Heads for the Black Hills,' 'Forrest Jr. Wins Top Honors at Film Fest.'

"Let's try that one," Rinnah suggested.

Meagen clicked the headline and after a moment, the full article appeared.

"Hmmm..." Meagen hummed. "Looks like he won some kind of film festival at USC when he was a senior there. That was three years ago."

"An action movie, yeah?" Tommy said with excitement.

"Sorry," she said. "It says here that it's a documentary." At that, Tommy rose from his crouching position in front of the computer and picked up his book on magic tricks.

"Let me know if you find anything interesting."

Rinnah went back to the article and continued reading.

"Says here that the award led to all kinds of offers from Hollywood. Wonder why he chose not to take them?"

Meagen shrugged her shoulders and finished reading the article. When Rinnah was done, they went back to the page of hits.

"Looks to me like that's the only article about Ben and not just a mention from an interview with his dad," Rinnah said. Then a thought struck her.

"Meagen, how far back were we searching?"

"Five years."

"Can we search farther back?"

"Yep. I'll just tell the engine to look back, say, 10 years?"

Rinnah nodded and Meagen worked the keyboard. After a moment, the results page loaded. It showed 54 hits.

"Yikes!" Meagen said. "He must have been in high school during some of these articles."

Meagen scrolled past the previous hits, and went to the earliest headlines.

Suddenly Rinnah froze.

"Oh my God!" she whispered when she read one of the earliest headlines.

Tommy looked up from his book. "Find something?"

Meagen found the headline Rinnah had read and gawked in disbelief.

"No wonder he was questioned!"

Rinnah then read the headline out loud so Tommy could hear.

"Woman Drowned in Famed Director's Pool. Teenaged Son Held for Questioning."

Rinnah stared at the headline, preparing herself for what kind of information the full article would provide. And what, she wondered, would that be? She thought to herself that there's only one way to find out.

"Click it."

BEN'S BIG SECRET

CHAPTER TWELVE

THERE WERE A TOTAL of eight articles in the database that covered the story, and pretty much all of them said the same thing.

On April 19th, eight years ago, 23-year-old Heidi Thompson was found dead and floating in Hank Forrest's pool. The director and his wife were on location for a movie and had left Ben home alone. From the tone of the article, Rinnah gathered that he often had the run of the Hollywood Hills mansion to himself.

The stories went on to say that Ben called 911 at around

4:30 P.M. During questioning, he had told police that he had been home from school nearly an hour before calling. He had not been out to the pool prior to the time he made that call.

"Sounds reasonable to me," Meagen said. "Making a bee-line to the swimming pool right after school might not be something he did that often."

"Yeah, I think so too," Rinnah replied. "But what I find so interesting is who this Heidi person was."

"She sounds kinda crazy, yeah?"

By this time, Tommy had squeezed in-between the girls and was reading the screen with them. He pointed to a paragraph in one of the stories.

"It says she was a college student who was stalking Hank," he read. "She wanted him to make some kind of movie. Guess she wasn't taking 'no' for an answer, yeah?"

The kids re-read the current article as Meagen scrolled down the screen. At the end of the story, Rinnah stood.

"Can you save these, Meagen, until we can get them printed?"

Meagen nodded and began selecting the articles to save in a folder she discreetly named "BF Docs."

"I'm starving!" Tommy announced as he stood from the floor.

"Let's see if Mrs. Lane has any plans for lunch."

Meagen looked up from her laptop and added, "You guys go ahead. I'll do some research on the city of Varna."

"Good idea," Rinnah nodded. She then followed Tommy into the kitchen where they found Mrs. Lane cutting up a watermelon.

"You're just in time," she sang. "I'm making a fruit salad."

Rinnah's mouth watered as she watched the large woman scoop melon into balls and add them to a big bowl that already contained fresh cantaloupe. Mrs. Lane's bracelets rattled musically as her fleshy arms worked the watermelon. The blouse Mrs. Lane wore was perfect for the task as it was decorated with cartoon images of sliced watermelon. Rinnah smiled and took a seat at the small kitchen table, already laid out with plates and napkins, while Tommy headed for the fridge and began pulling out cold cuts, cheese, and condiments.

Rinnah had a thought.

"Mrs. Lane," she began, "how well do you know Tina?"

Mrs. Lane continued scooping and glanced curiously at Rinnah.

"Oh, pretty well, I guess. You can't work with someone eight hours a day, five days a week without getting to know her pretty well. Why do you ask, sweetheart?"

Rinnah shrugged. "I was just wondering if she has many friends out here..."

Tommy glanced at Rinnah as he opened a loaf of bread. He realized what Rinnah was fishing for, and looked at Mrs. Lane to see if she would bite.

"Delightful girl! I'm sure she has many friends."

Rinnah and Tommy exchanged looks when he handed her a couple slices of bread.

"Think there's anyone, er, special?" Rinnah prodded.

Tommy screwed up his face and mouthed the word "lame" as Rinnah began spreading mayonnaise on her bread. She ignored him and worked on her sandwich while continuing to gaze at Mrs. Lane.

Mrs. Lane ran her hands under the faucet, grabbed a dishtowel, and sat at the table with Rinnah. Her face took on a mischievous glow.

"You know something, Princess? I think she does!" she whispered conspiratorially. "Just the other day, she received a bouquet of flowers at the gallery."

Mrs. Lane giggled with delight.

"And she was soooo embarrassed. Wouldn't let me read the card or even tell me whom they were from."

Rinnah glanced at Tommy, who continued assembling what was turning into a very large bologna, ham, turkey, and cheese sandwich. Triple-decker.

When Rinnah returned her gaze to Mrs. Lane, she found the woman frowning.

"What's up?" she asked.

Mrs. Lane shook her head and pursed her lips.

"It's just the way she acted. Not just embarrassed … something else. Like she was a little bit angry. And that's not all," she said, reaching for a bag of chips. With a strange look on her face, she opened it and poured the contents into a bowl. "It was something she said. The word she used when I went on and on about how beautiful that bouquet was."

Rinnah leaned forward. A slice of cheese dangled limply between her fingers as she waited for Mrs. Lane to go on.

"She said they were 'inappropriate, completely inappropriate.'"

"Hmmm," Rinnah replied. "What kind of flowers were they?"

Mrs. Lane's painted eyebrows flew up when she said, "Roses! Big, beautiful red ones."

Rinnah shot a curious glance at Tommy and found him struggling with his sandwich. She thought about the delivery of Tina's roses, wondering what *that* was all about, as she continued fixing lunch. When she finished a second sandwich for Meagen, a familiar face peered into the kitchen and caught Rinnah's attention.

"Grandfather!"

Rinnah leapt from her seat and threw her arms around

the old Indian man. He bent and stuck his cheek out for his granddaughter to kiss. She did so with a loud smack.

"Does this mean Dancer's here?"

Her grandfather replied with a chuckle. "Yes, he is. But I had to fight with your mother to bring him."

Rinnah looked puzzled.

"She heard about that foreign woman getting killed at the hospital and wanted you to come home."

Rinnah's heart skipped a beat, and she looked harder at her grandfather. Mrs. Lane stood from the table and clucked.

"Dreadful! I've been trying to put that awful business out of my mind all morning. What is this world coming to? I thought I would get away from all that when I moved from Washington."

Rinnah watched as Mrs. Lane puttered in the kitchen, looking for anything to do just to keep her hands busy. She knew what she meant when Mrs. Lane said "all that."

She meant murder.

And now it had come to Spearfish.

Rinnah remembered the look of fear in Cassandra's eyes as she told her that "They're after the Rose."

She made a silent vow to find out who killed her and to see that they paid for it.

And with that, an idea began to form in her mind.

SNEAKING THROUGH THE FOREST
CHAPTER THIRTEEN

"CAREFUL! THIS TRAIL is really narrow."

Rinnah guided Dancer with the reins she held in one hand, and finished off her sandwich with the other. Her backpack bounced with each step Dancer took, and was filled with detective tools, like her tiny, high-tech binoculars, archaeologists kit, camera, purple note pad and matching pencil, and a few of Mrs. Lane's oatmeal and chocolate-covered raisin cookies, just for good measure. Following a few cautious feet behind her, Meagen clung to Tommy as he munched a cookie. He pretty much let Buck

Eye, Meagen's horse, follow Dancer without much use of the reins at all. Buck Eye knew what he was doing, and gave a quick snort anytime he felt Meagen squirm in the saddle.

As soon as her grandfather brought the horses, Rinnah did some fast-talking with Mrs. Lane. Now the kids followed a winding stream through the Canyon, with the highway on one side and steep, wooded cliffs on the other. Occasionally, a trout would leap from the stream as it made its way to bigger waters, causing Meagen to shriek with delight. More than once, Tommy had to tell her to get a grip, as he was afraid Meagen would spook the horses.

"So, Meagen," Rinnah called out as she dug her heels into Dancer's flank, guiding the horse effortlessly over a fallen log. "Tell us what you were able to find out about Varna."

Meagen finished tying her blonde hair back with a pink scrunchie and answered loudly over the sound of a waterfall they were just passing.

"Well," she began. "I didn't have a whole lot of time, but I did find out that we wouldn't want to go there on vacation anytime soon."

Rinnah frowned and continued listening.

"There's a lot of political stuff going on. Like civil

unrest and junk. From what I could tell, the country used to be run by a monarchy about a hundred years ago. But the royals were de-throned in one of those palace coup thingies, like a mini Bastille Day. The king was killed, but his wife and daughter escaped with the help of some loyal servants. Which was just as well, because it was the queen who ruled anyway."

At this point, the gang had to cross the stream at one of its shallowest points to pick up the trail on the other side. Once they made it, Rinnah had a question.

"Why the civil unrest now?"

Tommy grunted. "What's with the history lesson? We're on summer vacation, yeah?"

Meagen ignored him and answered Rinnah. "'Cause there's this group of people that want the royalty back in power. They think that the original de-throning was a big political move by one of the royal advisors. And anyway, it looks like the current government is totally corrupt. Now the people want their queen back. Or at the very least, the jewels."

At this, Rinnah ordered Dancer to a quick stop.

"Jewels?!"

Buck Eye snorted and stopped just short of Dancer. Meagen's arms flailed as she righted herself on the saddle.

"Oh, yeah. Didn't I mention that?"

Rinnah shook her head. "No. And, hello! Major important detail."

"Well, OK," Meagen said. "Don't get your panties bunched."

Tommy laughed, and, after a moment, so did Rinnah.

"All right. Sorry about that. I guess I'm taking this teen detective thing waaaay seriously."

Meagen shrugged and said, "Well, someone *has* been killed..."

Rinnah and Tommy sobered up at that, as Meagen went on.

"When the queen and her daughter left, they took the royal jewels with them. The important piece is some necklace."

"Why's it important?" Tommy asked.

"It's worn instead of a crown," Meagen explained. "The necklace is only worn by the queen, and it has a lot of political importance attached to it. It's like a national treasure. But of course, it's lost. There are even a couple pages on the Web site devoted just to the royal jewels. I was able to find out that the centerpiece is this totally famous ruby. At least in Varna. It's supposed to be, like, the biggest ruby ever. Not only that, but it's cursed. There's major history behind it. Like the Hope Diamond, or something."

Rinnah paused a moment, then asked, "What were you able to find out about it?"

Meagen shook her head and repositioned herself on the saddle.

"Not much, except that they don't have any pictures of it or anything. I didn't get to read more than that. I was just about to when your grandfather showed up."

Rinnah lingered just a moment longer, then turned Dancer back around and pushed forward.

"Well, we can look into that later. We're here now, anyway."

As Dancer led the way, Tommy and Meagen exchanged a quick look. Finally, Tommy gave Buck Eye a gentle kick and caught up.

"Where's 'here'?"

Rinnah continued on in silence. Finally, she slowed Dancer to a stop in front of a row of giant lilacs. Their scent filled the air with sweet perfume, and Meagen found herself breathing in great lungfulls.

"Wow! I've never seen so many lilacs!"

Rinnah turned and put a finger to her lips. She then jumped down from Dancer and tied the reins to one of the bush's bigger branches. Tommy and Meagen followed suit, and joined Rinnah as she stepped between two of the largest bushes.

On the other side of the lilacs was a small cabin. There were no cars parked in the gravel drive, but Tommy and Meagen recognized the house from their drive into town earlier that morning.

"It's Ben's cabin!" Tommy said in a loud whisper.

"Yeah, I know," Rinnah replied. "I want to check something out."

As Tommy and Meagen reluctantly followed, Rinnah scurried toward the front door. Subconsciously, she gripped the medicine bag that hung from around her neck. Just as she reached the front door, a twig snapped somewhere in the distance.

"What was that?"

The kids froze on the front porch. Their eyes went toward the direction of the noise. To the lilacs. And the horses beyond.

"Just Dancer, yeah?" Tommy offered. "Or Buck Eye."

Satisfied with Tommy's explanation, Rinnah turned the knob of the front door. It was unlocked and gave way with a quiet squeak.

The kids slipped quietly into Ben's cabin, unaware that a dark figure, speaking softly into the flickering ears of Dancer and Buck Eye, watched every move they made.

THE TELL-TALE DOCUMENTARY

CHAPTER FOURTEEN

"THIS IS SO not right, Rinnah!"

Meagen stood just inside the tiny living room, while Rinnah walked around.

"The door was unlocked, so it's not like we're breaking and entering or anything," she answered. "Besides, if anyone catches us, we'll just say we got lost."

Meagen watched from the front door as Rinnah and Tommy scoped out the small cabin. At the opposite end of the wood-paneled living room was a sliding glass door that led out onto a small deck, which in turn overlooked a view of the winding creek and the rocky cliffs just beyond. In front of the glass slider sat a vintage Formica dining set with four matching chairs. The surface of the table was uncluttered, save for several books and a legal note pad.

"Text books?" Tommy cried in disgust. "What's up with that?"

"Sssshhhh!" Meagen hissed. "Someone will hear you!"

Tommy rolled his eyes, but fell silent. Meagen crossed her arms and tapped her foot while looking out the front door.

"We shouldn't be here," she said, almost to herself.

Rinnah ignored her and turned her attention back to the dining room table. She noticed one title read *Algebraic Fundamentals.* With a quick "hm," she turned from the table and walked through the open dining area and into the kitchen. It was a very small room, with an antique wood stove that, judging by the coffeepot and iron skillet that sat there, Ben used to cook with. Rinnah picked up the coffeepot, looked inside and noticed it was about half full. It was also cold, making Rinnah guess that Ben had been gone for some time. A small, wooden rack held the clean breakfast dishes and was draped with a small kitchen towel. The rest of the kitchen was spotless as well.

"Not the typical bachelor pad," Rinnah commented to herself.

She left the kitchen and was making her way through the living room when a thought struck. She stopped and her attention gravitated toward a pine entertainment center that housed a large TV.

"Check this out!"

Rinnah turned at the sound of Tommy's voice and found him pointing at a framed movie poster that hung on the wall above a roll top desk. When Meagen scowled, Tommy waved her off with a flapping hand.

Rinnah saw that the desk itself was cluttered with mail, pens, pocket change, and a small desk calendar with a picture of Mt. Rushmore printed above a grid of dated weeks. Something clicked in her brain, but the feeling left too quickly for Rinnah to pursue it.

"*Too Young to Die*," Meagen read when she decided to join Tommy and Rinnah at the desk. "That's appropriate."

Tommy ignored the black joke and continued gazing at the poster.

"It's signed by Hank Forrest!"

Meagen rolled her eyes and wandered over to a small couch that sat facing the entertainment center. She sat down with a cautious plop and looked around the room.

"What if he comes back?"

Rinnah began opening cabinets that surrounded the TV.

"We'll hear his truck pull up," she replied.

Meagen turned and kept her eyes on the front door. At her insistence, Rinnah kept it open. She kept watch on it now, ready to spring from the couch should Ben's truck come crunching along the gravel drive.

Rinnah continued poking through the cabinets and shelves that framed the TV set. She found several of Hank Forrest's movies on DVD and put them back on the shelf. Meagen took her eyes off the front drive and began to watch Rinnah as she rummaged through the videocassettes that lined the shelf under the TV.

"You're looking for something in particular, aren't you?" she asked after a few minutes.

"Yep," Rinnah replied. "I'm interested in that film Ben made for his senior project. I think it might tell us something about—bingo!"

Rinnah held up a dusty video and waved it in the air triumphantly. Tommy tore his eyes away from framed photos of Hank Forrest and joined Meagen on the sofa.

"It's that documentary, yeah?"

Rinnah turned on the TV and slid the tape into the VCR.

"Rinnah, don't. We're so gonna get caught!" Meagen jumped from the sofa and started for the door.

"Relax, Meagen. This'll only take a sec."

But Meagen didn't relax. Instead, she paced behind the

sofa, her eyes darting from the front door to the TV screen.

"My dad's gonna go ballistic if he finds out."

Rinnah hit the Fast Forward button on the remote until the blackness was replaced with a title card. Now that she found the beginning of the film, she hit Play.

"*The Curse of the Royal Ruby*," she read. Then, a subtitle appeared.

"The Story of the Other Anastasia."

"Anna who?" Tommy asked.

"Anastasia," Meagen answered, her eyes now lingering on the TV screen. "You know, that story of the Russian Tsar and his family that were killed by communist revolutionaries."

Rinnah and Tommy looked at her like she was from another planet.

"Well, it's an interesting story."

Tommy and Rinnah exchanged quick looks. Meagen ignored them and went on.

"Some people think that the daughter, Anastasia, got away with—"

"With the royal jewels!" Rinnah cried, remembering the story.

"Whoa!" Tommy whispered. "That's just like the story of the Varna queen."

Meagen now came back to the sofa and squeezed in between Tommy and Rinnah. Her eyes glowed with interest as she leaned forward and watched the flickering screen.

"So, who's this other Anastasia?"

The kids watched as the title card dissolved into an image of a great castle, which caused Meagen to gasp.

"That's the Palace of the Queen. In Varna!"

The sound of Ben's voice, as he began narrating the story, filled the room. He described the fall of the Bulgarian royals in 1915, and the ascension of a corrupt government that offered the equivalent of a $500,000 reward for the return of the royal jewels. The lives of the queen and her daughter need not be spared, just so long as the jewels are returned.

Then the film cut to a formal garden of exotic flowers and beautiful roses. The kids became enthralled as the story unfolded. Suddenly, the front door creaked, causing all three to turn in their seats.

The doorway was empty.

"Just the wind, yeah?" Tommy offered.

Meagen jumped up and ran to the front door. With both hands on the doorframe, she looked left, then right before turning back to her friends.

"No one," she said with an uneasy shrug. She took one

last look out the front door before joining Rinnah and Tommy on the small sofa. A wide shot of the garden filled the screen as a haunting melody played in the background.

"The botanical gardens…" Meagen murmured at the familiar sight. "I saw that when I was researching the Internet."

Ben, as narrator, began to describe the royal jewels as the camera panned through the rose garden.

"The legend of the royal jewels have reached Anastasian proportions. Even the Bulgarian Queen's name, Annabella, brings to mind the more famous story of Anastasia and the ultimate fairy tale that modern speculation has created."

The camera continued to move through the garden, past one rose bush after another. Rinnah found herself clasping again at the medicine bag her grandmother had given her and remembered with a chill the special item that had been put there. The rose petals. Ben's warm, deep voice continued as the camera moved throughout the garden.

"Let us examine one jewel in particular, so that we may fully understand its meaning to the Bulgarian Royals, to Queen Annabella and her daughter the Princess Lila, and, in fact, to the whole of Bulgaria. For some say that this priceless treasure of legendary beauty is, at its very heart, a symbol of power. It's been documented that only the queen herself wore the jewel. One story has it that a servant, during the reign of Queen Annabella's grandmother, once put on the jewel in a moment of thoughtless vanity and was discovered. She was executed at the guillotine for her lapse in royal etiquette."

The camera zoomed in and froze on one flawless red rose as Ben continued speaking. The frame slowly faded as another image grew in clarity. Finally, Rinnah could make out the lines of an exquisite necklace, the center of which she could still see the rose from the garden shot. As that rose faded completely, she found that she was staring at the centerpiece of a magnificent necklace circling the throat of a woman with the unmistakable bearing of a queen.

Rinnah gasped as she realized what she was looking at. A very old oil painting, the subject of which had to be the Queen of Varna.

"It's Annabella," Meagen said.

Rinnah gazed at the painting as Ben continued his narration. She chewed her bottom lip thoughtfully as she studied the Queen's necklace.

"The crown jewel," Ben was saying, "is the world's largest ruby, intricately carved by a master jeweler and the color of crimson, the color of blood. Fitting, given the stone's infamous and deadly past," he teased. After a beat, he continued.

"This is the only known portrait of Queen Annabella, and, interestingly enough, the only known picture of the Royal Ruby."

At that, the camera zoomed tighter still on the ruby, causing Rinnah to gasp.

"The Rose!"

Meagen's and Tommy's eyes went wide. Rinnah hit Pause on the remote and turned.

" 'They're after The Rose,' " she said, remembering the dead woman's words. "How absolutely unusual."

Meagen remained silent and stared at the frozen jewel that jittered on the TV screen. Rinnah looked at her and frowned.

"Meagen?" she asked. "What is it?"

Meagen tore her gaze away from the TV and locked her eyes on Rinnah.

"Ben," she mumbled.

"Yeah. I know. This is a major clue." Then, as Rinnah saw the anxious look in Meagen's eyes, she said, "But just because Ben did a documentary on The Rose, doesn't mean he killed anyone."

It was a lame statement. Rinnah knew it. And so did Meagen. The two continued gazing at each other until Rinnah finally looked away. She pushed the Play button and the video began rolling again.

"Art scholars believe that the Royal Ruby was the work of Count Vladimar, who designed all the royal jewelry in the late 18th century. Because of his taste for incorporating designs he found in the castle gardens, Queen Isabel, Annabella's great, great grandmother, dubbed him 'The Florist.'"

Rinnah paused the tape and began searching her bag.

"'The Florist!'" she said. "It's in the note!"

She found the note and read it again. "'They have sent the Florist.'"

Rinnah looked up from the note and hit Play, continuing the tape.

"Because of the ruby's unusual size and radiant color, a royal clergyman declared Vladimar's work to be that of the Devil's. So persuasive was his argument, that the jeweler was burned at the stake for witchcraft. But not before placing a curse on the necklace, and all who come in contact with it."

Rinnah shivered and felt the hairs on the back of her neck rise. She listened as Ben narrated more of the story.

"It is said that members of the castle staff died mysterious and horrible deaths. A cook's helper, who was known to be an intimate of Vladimar's, succumbed to massive burns when a pot of boiling fat flew from the cooking fire. An apprentice of Vladimar's, who assisted in the Royal

Ruby's creation, was found in his bed, stung to death by poisonous insects. The royal dressmaker took her own life by throwing herself in front of a carriage. The list goes on until no fewer than seven people died or went insane. And all of them had direct ties to the Royal Ruby."

Rinnah paused the tape and shot quick looks at Tommy and Meagen. She pulled out a pad and pencil and began making notes. Death. Insanity. Rinnah shivered at the thought. She began writing more and felt the air behind her move.

"This is totally freakin' me out," she whispered.

Tommy and Meagen sat with their eyes glued to the frozen images on the TV screen. Rinnah went back to her notebook and scribbled some more. She thought she heard a slight creaking of the hardwood floor. The side of her face grew warm and her scalp prickled with the tiniest twinges of fear. She tried shaking the feeling, but it wouldn't go away.

"Seven deaths attributed to the curse of the Royal Ruby," she said as she continued scribbling notes.

The couch jostled as Tommy shifted in his seat. Meagen crossed her legs and sighed. Rinnah reached for the remote. Another creak sounded as something moved behind her, the noise causing a tiny ripple in the silence of the cabin.

Rinnah froze. She felt it. A presence. In the room.

Slowly, Rinnah turned in her seat. Her heart began to pound as she saw movement out of the corner of her eye.

Someone stood at the threshold of the forgotten front door.

CAUGHT IN THE ACT

CHAPTER FIFTEEN

"WELL IF IT ISN'T the three little pigs."

Meagen yelped and jumped from the sofa. Rinnah and Tommy did the same and turned their attention to the front door.

Standing at the threshold of the cabin was Victor Little Horn. His leering gaze locked on Rinnah, freezing her to the spot.

"What are you doing here?" was all Rinnah could muster. With the remote hidden behind her back, she felt for the Off button and pushed it. She was surprised when Victor started laughing.

"What do you mean, what am *I* doing here? What are *you* doing here?"

He stopped laughing suddenly and stalked further into the room. He carried a backpack over his shoulder and tossed it to the floor when he reached the back of the sofa.

Rinnah felt her face go hot and wished her heart would stop pounding so wildly in her chest. As the silence filled the space between her and Victor, Rinnah started to become angry. Angry at getting caught, sure, but angry none the less.

"It's none of your business why I'm here!"

In her now agitated state, Rinnah had forgotten that she wasn't alone. Tommy and Meagen stood wide eyed and silent on either side of their friend, neither one daring to move until there was some sign that Victor wasn't going to leap over the sofa and beat them senseless.

Rinnah continued meeting Victor's stare, unaware that she clenched the medicine bag that hung from her neck.

Victor crossed his arms. He looked like a wooden Indian, standing there waiting for Rinnah to tell him why the kids were sitting on Ben's sofa like they owned the place. However, the anger that burned in Victor's eyes made him seem a lot more dangerous than a statue standing in front of a cigar store.

The anger slowly drained from Rinnah, and was replaced by curiosity.

"What were you——?"

Just then the front door closed, causing everyone, including Victor, to jump.

"Wow! Did I forget I was throwing a party?"

Ben Forrest smiled inquisitively from over Victor's beefy shoulder. His blue eyes, sparkling happily, landed on each of the kids as if to offer silent hellos. But when he stepped between Victor and the sofa, Rinnah could tell that Ben knew he had interrupted a potentially bloody situation.

"Sorry I'm late, Victor," he said as he continued looking at Rinnah. "I had an errand to run."

Victor glared at Rinnah. Then, in one fluid motion, he reached over the back of the sofa and snatched the remote from her hand. Rinnah snarled and leaned one knee on a sofa cushion. She reached up for the remote, but Victor held it over his head. Without taking his eyes from Rinnah, he began growling accusations.

"These little brats broke into your house," he began. Rinnah noticed that one of Ben's eyebrows raised, but the smile that played across his lips seemed to indicate that he found the situation more comical than anything else. He remained silent, allowing Victor to go on.

"Looks like they were sizing up some of your video equipment. Nosy little hypocrite!" he said to Rinnah. "Why do people put up with you?"

Anger flashed brightly in Rinnah's eyes. Before she could fire off a retort, Ben spoke.

"Oh, I know why you're here!" he said. "I have the lease ready to go." With that, Ben walked across the room to the desk and began to rummage. "Tell your dad I'm sorry I didn't get this signed and back to him sooner."

Ben returned to the sofa and handed Meagen a legal sized envelope bulging with hastily folded materials.

"That should put us square."

Victor grimaced and turned away from Rinnah. She could tell that they all knew she wasn't in Ben's cabin to retrieve a rental agreement. And that it really ticked Victor off.

"Would anyone like something to drink?" Ben asked with a smile. He turned and walked into the small kitchen. Victor threw down the remote with a huff and followed Ben out of the room.

"Whew!" Tommy breathed. "That was close, yeah?"

Rinnah moved fast. She picked up the remote and pushed a button, causing the VCR to whir back into life. The tape ejected, and she dashed to the machine and removed it from the slot. She could hear Victor's vicious whispering coming from the kitchen as she shoved the tape into her bag.

"Rinnah!" Meagen hissed. "What are you doing?"

Rinnah shushed Meagen with a frown. At that moment, Ben returned to the living room displaying a plastic jug as if he were in a commercial.

"I have orange juice?..."

Rinnah cinched her bag tightly. "Uh ... no thanks. We should really be getting back."

Ben shrugged and Rinnah pushed at Tommy and Meagen in an effort to break their stupor. They finally moved and allowed themselves to be herded toward the door.

Victor came back out of the kitchen and slunk toward the desk. He crossed his arms and shot Rinnah an angry scowl as he leaned against the doorjamb. Rinnah let her eyes stray from Victor's and began to scan the desk once more. She saw the calendar and gasped.

"Oh my God!"

Then she felt herself being pulled roughly through the cabin's front door and looked up to see Meagen looking more than a little bit angry.

"Let's GO!" she mouthed silently.

Rinnah's head was spinning as they walked across the gravel drive and back to their horses. When they got there, Tommy helped Meagen onto Buck Eye and peered at Rinnah curiously when he settled himself onto the horse's back.

"What's up with you?" he asked as he tightened the reins.

Rinnah jumped onto Dancer and turned the horse around to face Tommy and Meagen.

"The note!" she gasped. "I know what it all means!"

DECIPHERING A MESSAGE

CHAPTER SIXTEEN

"IT ALL MAKES sense now!" Rinnah was saying as she dug through her bag. She let Dancer lead the way back to the cabin without any help from her at the reins. Buck Eye followed closely behind as Tommy and Meagen leaned forward in an effort to hear every word Rinnah was saying.

"It came to me when I saw the desktop calendar back at Ben's."

Finally, Rinnah pulled the note free and read it aloud once more.

"'The time has come for our independence.' That means July 4th. And the 'exploding heavens' means a fireworks show. But the part that didn't make sense, until I saw that calendar, was 'Take care under their stony gaze.'"

Rinnah turned in the saddle to look Tommy and Meagen in the eye.

"'Stony gaze.' Get it?"

Tommy and Meagen exchanged a pained glance. Rinnah turned back around in her saddle with a shake of her head.

"Mt. Rushmore!" she exclaimed. "Something's gonna happen during the Fourth of July fireworks show at Mt. Rushmore!"

Tommy thought for a moment, then asked Rinnah a question as he and Meagen ducked their heads to avoid a stray evergreen bough.

"What do you think is gonna happen?"

Rinnah pursed her lips, thinking. Finally her eyes got wide.

"I'll bet it has something to do with the Rose. Maybe it's some kind of ultra-secret meeting." Rinnah paused and thought some more. "This 'Sage' person gave the note to Lily as a coded, secret message to tell her the time and place to meet."

"At Mt. Rushmore during the Fourth of July fireworks show."

"That's right, Meagen," Rinnah said. "And I know what to do."

Meagen and Tommy exchanged worried glances.

"What are you gonna do?" Tommy asked.

Rinnah kicked Dancer's flank to speed him up a bit.

"Well, investigate the fireworks show, of course."

"What?!" Tommy cried.

Rinnah clucked impatiently.

"Gimme a break, Tommy. I probably won't even be able to find this Sage person, so it'll probably be a bust. But, just in case," Rinnah continued, "Maybe I will, and I can find out what the meeting is for. I'll bet Sage knows something about the Royal Ruby, something that might lead me to Lily's killer. After all, Ben's video said that those are some major jewels. Definitely worth enough to kill for. We're talking really big money."

"Worth more than that," Meagen muttered from her precarious position atop Buck Eye. Rinnah turned around.

"What do you mean?"

"Well, the video said that the necklace meant more to the people of Varna than just money. There's all kinds of political junk attached to it. The woman who wears that necklace isn't just a queen. She's the most politically powerful person in the country. And the only thing that causes someone to kill more often than money is..."

Rinnah turned back around in the saddle and finished the thought.

"...is power."

*   *   *

When the kids arrived back to the cabin, they found Tina seated comfortably in a leather chair while Mrs. Lane scurried from room to room, tidying and gathering clutter.

"Hey, Tina!"

Tina looked around at the sound of Meagen's voice. When she saw the kids enter the room, she smiled and waved.

"Hey, guys. What's going on?"

Rinnah smiled at the young woman, but inside she frowned.

"We thought you were headed back to the gallery…" Rinnah said, trying to sound casual. The smile on Tina's face froze for just a moment. Then she answered, matching Rinnah's casual tone with one of her own.

"I thought I would come back out and spend an afternoon playing tourist. Hope you don't mind."

"Not even," Tommy said. "What should we do?"

Mrs. Lane poked her head out from the girls' room and fluttered a fleshy hand.

"If we hurry, we can just get to the park in time for the Sioux Memorial dedication."

As Mrs. Lane disappeared back into the bedroom, Tina stood and gathered her purse and a light sweater from the coffee table.

"Sounds good to me."

Other than the slight pause when confronted with her change in plans, Rinnah could find no trace of Tina's odd behavior of that morning. In fact, she acted as if that morning didn't even happen.

"Yeah," Rinnah agreed, thinking of the fish hatchery located within the park. "Me, too."

Mrs. Lane charged back into the living room, talking to herself as she searched for her hand bag and an appropriate hat.

"I've got the Crock Pot loaded, so dinner should be ready when we return. There's not enough for a full load of laundry yet, but I still should talk to Bill about his shirts. Oh, where are my sunglasses?" Tommy rolled his eyes as Rinnah and Meagen chuckled to themselves. Tina checked her watch.

"We should have plenty of time, Mrs. Lane."

Rinnah noticed the henna tattoo again on the back of her hand. Just as a thought began to form in Rinnah's mind, Mrs. Lane came up behind her.

"I'm as ready as I'll every be," she sang. Rinnah looked up and noticed another huge hat had appeared on Mrs. Lane's head, this one in bright orange with a flowing scarf attached to the back that floated behind the large woman like a yellow piggy-backing ghost.

Once inside Mrs. Lane's Cadillac, Rinnah tried chasing down the thoughts that began to play hide and seek within her mind when she saw Tina's tattoo. After a while, she gave up and gazed out the car window at the beautiful, forest-like scenery that flew past.

After finding a parking space a couple blocks away from the park, Rinnah and the rest of the gang arrived at the makeshift stage just as an official from the Chamber of Commerce was finishing Katharine Black Elk's introduction. A large screen made of muslin blocked the Memorial from view of the crowd and stood just to the right of the stage.

"Isn't she just beautiful?" cried Mrs. Lane when the high school senior took the stage. "So exotic looking."

As Mrs. Lane held her digital camera above the people in front of her, Rinnah scanned the crowd for the girl's grandfather, Ronnie Black Elk. Finally, she found him, beaming proudly from the side of the stage.

Katharine stepped up to the microphone, causing a screech of feedback. The audience tittered, and Katharine looked at a scruffy looking teen who immediately began checking cords and sliding knobs, looking like he hadn't a clue.

"Thank you all for coming to this dedication service," Katharine began meekly. When it appeared that she would encounter no further technical difficulties, Katharine's voice became more confident.

"I am truly honored to be chosen to introduce the Sioux Memorial. Generations of great Sioux leaders were born here. They lived, raised families, fought for their tribe— and later for their country—and eventually died here, making the Black Hills a spiritual and cultural center for the Sioux people. And this tribute to them will help us all remember the mighty warriors that made this place our home. Like the Great Spirit, our ancestors will never leave us, for their memory will last forever."

A smattering of applause, led by Mrs. Lane, rippled through the crowd. Rinnah looked up to see the woman's hat flapping up and down as she nodded in agreement. She occasionally sighed and dabbed tears from her eyes. When it became silent again, Katharine went on.

"A very wise man, a Sioux medicine man, once told me that it isn't blood that makes a person Sioux. It isn't the feather in her hair, or the brown eyes, or the red skin. It is the way she lives her life. With pride, dignity, and rever-ence for life itself, in all its forms. That man was my grandfather, Mr. Ronnie Black Elk. And it is people like my grandfather whom this memorial sets out to celebrate by making you and me remember the greatness of the Sioux people. To give us all the courage and the strength to make the ideals this memorial represents a part of who we are. Whether you are Sioux or not."

This got some big applause from the crowd, but Rinnah found the speech a little odd. She felt the crushing grip of Mrs. Lane as the woman hugged her close.

"Beautiful!" she sniffled.

Rinnah craned her neck and saw Tommy and Meagen smashed in on the other side. Tommy seemed to be gasping for breath, while Meagen smiled and patted the woman with a free hand.

"And now, I present to you a Memorial to the Sioux people."

The screen was pulled away by the Chamber of Commerce guy to reveal a massive boulder carved into the likeness of a traditional Sioux shield. The crowd oohed and aahed at the sight. Mrs. Lane let the kids go and the gang jostled forward for a closer look.

A small, brass plaque labeled the piece "Spearfish Sioux Memorial. Honoring the Men and Women of the Great Sioux Nation." Today's date ran just below the inscription.

"Hm!"

Rinnah turned to Tommy and found him looking sour-faced.

"What?" she asked.

Tommy shook his head and smirked. "The whites came

and took our hills, and all we get is this stupid little plaque, yeah?"

Just as Rinnah was shushing Tommy, a deep voice came from just over her shoulder and interrupted.

"Let the warrior have his opinions, Rinnah."

The kids looked up and found Ronnie Black Elk looking amused. He stepped closer to the monument and ran a large, deeply tanned hand over the carving. A beaded watchband peeked out from under the cuff of his denim shirt. As his hand slid farther up the stone, Rinnah could just make out a familiar design in the cut-glass beads. Startled, she glanced up and her eyes met those of her medicine man. He smiled down on her, as if he knew what she was thinking.

Rinnah looked away and smiled a greeting at Katharine as she stepped forward to inspect the monument, but her thoughts remained on Ronnie Black Elk's watchband. The way the sun made the cut-glass beads of the design glow seemed almost supernatural. But that wasn't what made Rinnah start. It was the design itself—a rose so red, it was the color of blood.

Or the color of a ruby.

A CONFESSION OVER SCRAMBLED EGGS
CHAPTER SEVENTEEN

RINNAH PICKED AT her scrambled eggs and watched Tommy shove a red scarf into the fist of his hand. He opened it, and the wad of material fell to the table, just missing his bowl of cereal. With a scowl, he went back to his open magic book and flipped through the pages.

It was Monday morning, and Rinnah couldn't get the strange conversation she had had with Katharine Black Elk after the Sioux memorial dedication ceremony the day before, or the image of Ronnie Black Elk's beaded rose, out of her mind. She absently fingered the medicine bag that hung around her neck, trying to feel the rose petals the medicine man put in there. Mrs. Lane hummed loudly as she washed dishes in the sink, making Rinnah wonder where all the dirty dishes keep coming from. The woman seemed to always be elbow deep in hot water, her pudgy hands sheathed in yellow latex. Rinnah watched as Tommy got up from the table, poured some orange juice into a glass, gulped until it was empty, and then set the dirty glass back down on the counter.

"Well, that's one mystery solved." Mr. Paige sipped coffee and read the morning paper. From across the table, Rinnah could just make out the bold headline.

"Foreign Woman Murdered in Hospital Bed."

Rinnah knew the story by heart so she didn't ask to read the paper when Meagen's dad pushed it aside. Instead, she remembered how Ronnie Black Elk had taken up a friendly conversation with Mrs. Lane just as his granddaughter had stepped forward to check out the memorial stone.

"So, Rinnah, what do you think?" Katharine had asked with a bright smile.

"Pretty cool," Rinnah remembered responding, without much enthusiasm. Katharine caught her lack of interest and became curious.

"You think so?" she asked.

By that time, Rinnah had begun to stare at Ronnie Black Elk, or actually, his watchband. Katharine caught the gaze and followed it.

"My grandfather is so proud, it's like I'm afraid I'm going to disappoint him somehow, you know?"

Rinnah nodded. Then she asked Katharine a question. "What did you mean in your speech when you said that it isn't blood that makes a man Sioux?"

Katharine regarded Rinnah with curiosity.

"I mean, what you said your grandfather said?" Rinnah asked.

"I don't understand…"

"It's just that…" Rinnah paused, thinking out her question. Then she tried again. "Our people are so proud of our Indian blood. You know, coming off the Rez and being part of the white world, we're constantly being told that our Indian blood is the source of our strength and stuff like that. But your grandfather doesn't seem to agree with that much."

Katharine smiled and instantly understood what Rinnah had been trying to get at.

"My grandfather has many white friends that have taken on the Indian way of life. And you know how some of the tribes have taken in a white person in the past—"

"Stands with a Fist!"

Katharine looked puzzled at Rinnah's interruption.

"You know, from that movie *Dances with Wolves*. When they took in that little white girl and she grew up to be an Indian."

Katharine laughed.

"Yeah, just like that. My grandfather believes that it's sometimes your way of life more than your blood that makes you Indian. After all, look at all the different names that have come from the Rez. Vasquez. Williams. Even Jones. Those names are from white men that came to live with the Indian generations ago."

Something triggered within Rinnah, something just out of reach. She tried to capture it now, at the breakfast table, as Mrs. Lane scuttled about in the kitchen, and Tommy read from a magic book while munching toast. Soon, the sound of Mr. Paige's voice brought Rinnah out of her reverie.

"Where's Meagen?" he asked, glancing at his watch. Rinnah cleared the cobwebs from her mind and answered.

"Still in the shower, I think."

Mr. Paige frowned slightly and stood.

"Well, I've got to get to work. When you see her, would you please tell her not to be late?"

Rinnah looked puzzled.

"She's meeting me and Sandy for lunch today, and she

needs to be on time," he said, slightly distracted as he searched under a chair for his briefcase.

Rinnah blinked, a little surprised that Meagen didn't mention the lunch to her. Mr. Paige rose from his chair with his briefcase in one hand and smiled as Mrs. Lane took the coffee cup he balanced in the other.

"I can have someone come in and do the cleaning," he said as Mrs. Lane put the cup in the sink. "You're family now, not our maid."

Mrs. Lane wiped her hands on a bright orange dishtowel and poured herself the last of the coffee into her own cup. She then took it to the table where she sat next to Rinnah.

"You know, we had a maid when we lived in Washington," she said.

Tommy looked up from his book and grinned. "That must have been great! I've been trying to talk my folks into getting one for years."

Mrs. Lane chuckled and patted Tommy's hand.

"It was. She was such a hard worker, Maria was, and kept our home spotless. But we never had children, so there wasn't a whole lot of work for her to do. Even after Mr. Lane passed, I kept her on to take care of things at home while I set out to see the world."

Tommy's eyes lit up at the mention of globetrotting,

and he sat forward in his chair, eager to hear tales of wild adventure. He closed his book and pushed it to the side.

"I traveled for years after the Senator died. Cruises, cross-country train tours, midnight flights to God knows where—I did it all. And the shopping! I spent a fortune filling my house with trinkets from so many countries I can't even remember them all. I think I take the prize for the longest shopping spree in history."

She paused and took another sip of her coffee. When she set the cup back down with a small clunk on the wooden table, her eyes took on a kind of sadness that settled over her face like a shadow.

"It took me that long to realize I was just running away."

Tommy looked puzzled and fidgeted in his chair.

"Running away from what?"

Mrs. Lane smiled, her eyes shining bright with unshed tears.

"From the loneliness of a big, clean, empty house."

Rinnah felt a tug at her heart and glanced at Mr. Paige. He laid a hand on the large woman's shoulder and gave a gentle squeeze.

"I finally sold the house and let Maria go."

Mrs. Lane looked at Mr. Paige, with his briefcase and rumpled suit jacket clutched in one hand, and blinked away the tears.

"I like having a family to take care of."

Mr. Paige smiled, gave one final squeeze to Mrs. Lane's shoulder, and left the kitchen.

Rinnah and Tommy remained silent, listening to the sound of the Jeep starting up and crunching down the gravel drive toward the highway. The silence lingered on until Tommy finally broke it.

"Well then, you should come live with me, yeah?"

Rinnah gave Tommy a quick kick under the table as Mrs. Lane laughed and rose from her seat.

"Ow! Enough with the kicking already!"

Meagen entered the kitchen as Mrs. Lane stood from the table and busied herself with a few kitchen chores. Rinnah was about to offer her friend a quick, "Good morning," but Tommy cut her off.

"Yikes!" he said. "When's the beauty pageant?"

Meagen turned and that's when Rinnah noticed the lipstick, blush, and eyeshadow that painted Meagen's face. Rinnah shot Tommy a look that caused him to swing his legs out from under the table and hike them onto his chair. Meagen turned her back on Tommy and made her way to the kitchen counter. Rinnah decided not to say anything about the make up, at least with Tommy around.

"So what's up with lunch today?" she asked instead.

Meagen rolled her eyes and began making a fresh pot of coffee.

"Dad wants me to meet him and She-Geek at the hospital."

Mrs. Lane paused from her condiment shuffling in the pantry to shoot Meagen a disapproving look. From her vantagepoint at the kitchen counter, Meagen missed it. But Rinnah and Tommy didn't.

"You don't like Sandy?" Tommy asked.

Meagen snorted and sat down next to Rinnah at the table. She plucked a cold piece of toast from Rinnah's plate and nibbled while waiting for the coffee to finish brewing.

"Who said I didn't like her?"

Rinnah frowned and pushed her plate toward Meagen. Tommy shook his head and began flipping through the magic book.

"She's not that bad," Rinnah offered.

Meagen sighed in exasperation.

"What. Ever."

Meagen rose from her chair and went to the cupboard for a coffee mug.

"What's the plan today?" she asked.

Rinnah answered, but wasn't quite ready to let the matter of Sandy Price drop so quickly.

"Well, I was thinking of going back to check out the Wild West Days. Which should work out for you, 'cause it's so close to the hospital."

Meagen didn't bite. She removed the glass pot from the

167

coffee maker and put her cup underneath the steaming stream.

"You know, I should snoop around that place myself," she said as she waited for her cup to fill. "Somebody got to Lily and killed her. Maybe it was someone who worked there."

Mrs. Lane turned with an armful of dirty dishtowels and said, "Such gruesome talk for a little girl." She left the kitchen and headed for the laundry room. Meagen ignored her and continued.

"In fact, I've been thinking about it, and who better than the hospital administrator?"

Tommy looked up from his magic book.

"What are you talking about?" he asked.

Rinnah watched Meagen remove her coffee cup and replace it with the pot. Her mind went back to the gathering at Dirty Eddy's.

"Well, it's true. She can go anywhere in that place and nobody would think twice."

Rinnah felt goosebumps rise on her arms when she remembered talking about her last vacation. Her vacation in Europe.

As incredible as it sounded, Rinnah couldn't help but wonder.

Did Sandy Price kill Lily in her own hospital?

FINDING COMMON GROUNDS

CHAPTER EIGHTEEN

RINNAH STOOD AT a railing overlooking the fishpond and remembered her encounter with Lily the day of the race. She turned and examined the restroom entrance, forcing her mind to remember some small detail about the figure she saw standing there that day.

"It's no use," she said at last. "I'm not remembering anything."

Meagen finished applying lip gloss and checked her watch.

"That's OK," she said. "I have to get going, anyway."

Rinnah moved away from the railing and joined Meagen on the other side of the platform. Tommy threw pieces of stale bread from a large bakery loaf at the hungry fish.

"What a joke," Meagen said. "School's out for summer, and I'm still eating lunch at the caf."

Rinnah chuckled at the thought of eating at the hospital cantina, but thought Meagen seemed to be handling it pretty well.

"Come on, Tom," Meagen called. "It's time for me to get to the hospital."

Tommy dropped the entire loaf of bread into the pond with a loud splash and joined the girls.

Soon, the kids were walking down Main Street, past Dirty Eddy's and other shops. Meagen made a point of stopping to chat with shopkeepers that sat on benches in front of their stores. Twice, Rinnah had to remind Meagen that she was going to make herself late for lunch with her dad.

"Mrs. Lane's supposed to meet me and Tommy at the coffee house," she finally said to get Meagen moving. They were standing in front of an antique shop while Meagen pretended to be interested in an old mixing bowl displayed in the front window. "I don't want to keep her waiting."

Meagen huffed and turned to walk away.

"Oh, whatever," she said.

Just as they got to Common Grounds, the door opened and Ben Forrest stepped out. He wore jeans covered in sawdust and a sweaty T-shirt. In his left hand, he held a large coffee cup with "Common Grounds" emblazoned on a brown cardboard sleeve. His right hand was busy flipping open a pair of sunglasses, which he put on with a dazzling smile when he saw the kids.

"Hey, Ben!" Meagen called. She skipped toward him, but stumbled just within reach. Ben's free hand shot out and steadied the girl while coffee splashed out of his cup and splattered the sidewalk.

"Oops!" Meagen said when she regained her footing.

Tommy grabbed Rinnah's arm

"Oh, God!" he whispered. "Someone put her out of our misery."

Rinnah gave him a quick, but harmless, jab with her elbow. She picked up her pace and headed toward Ben as Meagen continued gazing into his eyes. Or was she just checking her make up in the reflection of his sunglasses? Rinnah wasn't sure.

"Hi," Rinnah said when she and Tommy reached Ben.

"Hey, Rinnah," he answered. "And Tommy ... just the man I want to see."

Meagen frowned, but Tommy's eyes lit up at the mention of his name.

"Yeah?"

"Oh, yeah," Ben said. "I just got a DVD of my dad's new movie, *Excessive Force*. Thought you might like to borrow it."

Tommy gasped.

"That's not even at the movies yet!" he cried. Then, looking at Rinnah, he yelled, "Score!"

Rinnah laughed and shook her head. Just then, the bell that hung from the coffee house door clanged. Rinnah looked up and found Victor Little Horn chewing on a muffin and gulping a Coke. When he saw Rinnah and Tommy, he snorted. Small bits of half-chewed blueberries flew from his mouth. Tommy gave an identical snort and turned away.

"So what are you guys up to today?" Ben asked before Victor could toss an insult. Rinnah decided it was time to hit the road, before things with Tommy and Victor got ugly. Again.

"We're just walking Meagen to the hospital. She's gonna be late for lunch with her dad."

Meagen scowled and crossed her arms. At the sight of Meagen, Victor grunted.

"What'd ya do to your face, Snow White?" he asked with a sneer. Then, with a quick glance at Ben, he said "Oh. I know. You're looking for Prince Charming." He then laughed, choking between gulps of Coke.

"Shut up, Victor!" Rinnah said. She didn't notice Mrs. Lane's yellow Cadillac as it pulled up and parked in front of the coffeehouse. But she did see Victor suddenly become quiet and glare hard over her shoulder. She turned around and saw Tina Treadwell closing the car door. As Mrs. Lane's assistant stepped up to the sidewalk, Rinnah looked at Ben to see his reaction. He merely sipped his coffee and said nothing.

"Uh ... hey, Tina," Rinnah said. "I thought Mrs. Lane was coming to get us."

Tina offered the group a tight smile before answering.

"She's on the phone with a new artist she hopes to wrangle for the gallery," she said. "I told her I would come out here and pick you up so she could talk to him without rushing."

The group fell into silence. Rinnah glanced around at everyone standing there. Even under the rouge, Rinnah could see Meagen's cheeks burning from Victor's remark. Tommy glowered at Victor, willing him to say something more so he could shoot some hurtful remark his way. Ben acted like he was reading a sign posted to the Common Grounds door announcing the book signing of an author Rinnah never heard of. When she got to Victor, she paused. He did nothing to hide a look of contempt.

He doesn't like Tina.

Finally, Rinnah broke the uncomfortable silence that held her friends glued to the sidewalk.

"Meagen, your dad's waiting."

With all eyes suddenly on her, Meagen moved away from the group in tiny, self-conscious steps.

"Yeah, he is," she said. "I guess I'll get going." Then, with a now shy glance to Ben, she said, "See ya later."

Victor burped and brushed past Tommy saying, "Time to get clocked in, bro."

Ben turned away from the small poster.

"Yeah, right. Let's go."

Without looking at Tina, Ben walked away. After a few steps, he turned back.

"Hey, Tommy," he called. "I'll get that movie to you later."

Tommy waved back and nodded. He then looked at Tina. "Guess we better get back, yeah?"

Tina nodded and made her way back to the car. As she got in, Rinnah noticed that Tina stared at Ben as he crossed the street. Victor caught her gaze and sneered.

Rinnah got in the back seat with Tommy.

"*That* was weird."

MEAGAN'S MELTDOWN

CHAPTER NINETEEN

WHILE MEAGEN WAS still at lunch, Rinnah reviewed printouts of the news clippings they had downloaded about the dead woman in Ben's pool. Other than reading that the director had been granted a restraining order against the girl, Rinnah learned nothing new.

On the coffee table sat her plate from lunch. A few crusts from her grilled cheese sandwich lay among potato chip crumbs. That and an empty juice glass lay waiting for Mrs. Lane's cleaning hands to come and swipe the items from the table and deposit them into a sink full of hot, soapy water.

Meagen's laptop lay open next to the juice glass. Rinnah had been examining the Web sites Meagen had bookmarked that detailed Varna, the queen, and the Royal Ruby. She sighed, thinking that there wasn't anything new to be discovered there either. Then her pulse quickened at the thought of Wednesday night's fireworks show at Mt. Rushmore.

"The time has come for our independence," Rinnah whispered aloud. Tommy looked up from his magic book, magician's cape twisted over his shoulder, as he tapped the chewed tip of his wand against his chin.

"Huh?" he asked.

Rinnah pulled her bag to her side and pulled out the note.

"Oh, I'm just wishing the Fourth of July would get here already."

Tommy grunted and Rinnah pulled the note from its matching envelope. She read it again.

Lily —
The time has come for our independence. Take great care under their stony gaze, for the exploding heavens shall illuminate our deeds. They've sent the Florist -- they know we are here and are after the Rose.
 — Sage

Rinnah mulled over the mention of the Florist and wondered what part this person was playing in the mystery. She put the note away after thinking awhile about Lily, Sage, and the Florist. She glanced at the digital clock glowing from desktop of Meagen's computer.

"I wonder how Meagen's big lunch is going," she said.

Tommy only grunted and Rinnah watched as he tried to do some trick with a quarter.

Rinnah pulled her legs up under her and sat back in the sofa. She remembered how Meagen had mentioned her belief that Sandy could have killed Lily while working at the hospital. Rinnah thought that there's no way Meagen could believe that, no matter how much she disliked her father's new friend. The fact that Sandy had gone to Europe on vacation was just a coincidence. Millions of people vacation in Europe every year. That doesn't mean Sandy knew anything about Varna, or the Queen, or even the Royal Ruby.

As if on cue, Rinnah heard the sound of Mr. Paige's Jeep crawl down the driveway. She looked out the window and saw Meagen jump from the vehicle and slam the door. The Jeep pulled away a little too fast, sending stray gravel flying behind the rear wheels.

"Uh oh."

Meagen came into the living room and threw herself upon the sofa.

"That was a total disaster."

Rinnah grabbed a pillow and put it in her lap. She leaned forward and gave Meagen her full attention.

"What happened?" she asked.

Meagen sighed and twisted her blonde hair into coils around her fingers.

"Well, it all started when I asked She-Geek—"

"Sandy," Rinnah interrupted.

"Whatever," Meagen said with a frown. "Anyway, I asked her about the day that Lily was killed—"

"You didn't!"

"I did!"

Rinnah shook her head.

"Well," Meagen said. "*I* think there's something evil about her. So I asked her what she was doing at the time Lily was killed. That's when my dad got all bent out of shape. He wigged, right there in the cafeteria. This one doctor, looking totally hot in his lab-coat, got up and—"

Rinnah sighed in exasperation, cutting Meagen off.

"Meagen, there's nothing evil about Sandy."

By this time, Tommy had given up on the quarter trick and entered the conversation.

"I think Rinnah's right, Meg," he said. "I just can't picture Sandy Price shoving a pillow over someone's face until they died."

Meagen stopped twisting her hair and threw her hands into the air.

"What's up with you guys?" she cried. "Whose side are you on, anyway?"

Rinnah grabbed the ends of the pillow and squeezed.

"We're on *your* side, Meagen. But you're freakin' out over nothing."

"I am so not freaking out," she argued. But her face turned red, and her pink, lip-glossed mouth twisted angrily. "You're just being too stupid to look at the right clues," Meagen argued.

Rinnah told herself to keep calm. When she could speak without her voice quivering, she said, "Then you're getting too emotional to—"

"To what?" Meagen yelled. "To see straight? To see that my dad is turning into a dork over his boss? That's easy for you to say. When was the last time your mom brought home a replacement for your dad?"

Rinnah gazed at her friend, not knowing how to respond. The remark hurt, and she had to will herself not to respond with further insults.

"She hasn't yet, but I'm sure I would be happy for her if she did make a new friend."

"Yeah, right," Meagen spat. "Until then, you can fill your time with inventing mysteries to solve so you don't have to deal with the fact that your dad's dead and your mom's gonna find you a new one any day now."

Rinnah felt her face burn and saw Tommy slouching in his chair. When she turned back to Meagen, she saw some-one standing on the front porch through the open window. Sandy Price. Wondering how much she heard, Rinnah got up from the sofa and opened the door.

"Hey, Sandy."

Sandy's cheeks were pink and she hesitated at the doorstep. Rinnah knew immediately that she had heard everything.

"Come in," Rinnah said. Her voice cracked and she tried clearing her throat as she led the woman in.

"I just came by to talk to Meagen," Sandy explained. Meagen rolled her eyes, making Rinnah embarrassed by her friend's behavior. Sandy looked at Meagen, and Rinnah noticed the hurt in the woman's eyes.

"Is there somewhere that you and I can talk in private, Meagen?"

Meagen shrugged her shoulders. "Right here's fine," she said.

Sandy looked around the room and seemed to become embarrassed herself. Rinnah gave Tommy a look that said they should find something else to do. When he stood from his seat, Meagen asked him to stay.

"These are my friends," she explained to Sandy.

"Well, you're definitely not acting like it," Rinnah said. Meagen looked at her and pleaded with her eyes for her to stay.

"It's OK," Sandy said. "Please stay. I promise I won't be long. I have to get back to work soon, anyway." When Rinnah looked unconvinced, Sandy nodded and gestured for her to take a seat. Then Sandy sat herself, looked at Meagen, and spoke.

"Meagen, I'm not here to be a replacement, dorky or otherwise."

Meagen looked a little surprised that Sandy had heard her, but said nothing. Sandy went on.

"I had a son that would be your age right about now," she said. "But he died of leukemia."

Meagen looked at her hands and pretended like what she was hearing didn't mean anything to her, but Rinnah saw the look on her face and knew it threw her off balance. Tommy wriggled in his seat, clearly uncomfortable by the revelation. With a look of determination, Sandy went on.

"My husband couldn't handle it. He drifted from me, from his whole family. His grief ate a hole in him, and nothing I could say or do could fill that emptiness."

Sandy paused and took a deep breath. She looked

around the room, remembering a very difficult time in her life, yet sharing it with Meagen and her friends like it was a movie, or something that happened to someone else, Rinnah thought. Finally, Sandy continued.

"He killed himself by taking a bottle of prescription medication the doctors gave him to help him sleep."

Rinnah heard Tommy gasp, but didn't look up. She was struggling with her own pain at hearing the deep sorrow that came with Sandy's words.

"I was working in the emergency room when they brought him in," she said. "He died in my arms, and there wasn't anything I could do to save him. Or my son, Danny."

With a deep sigh, Sandy Price stood from her chair and looked hard at Meagen.

"I'm not telling you this to make you feel sorry for me, so that you might like me. I'm telling you this only as an explanation of who I am." Then she paused, and the lines of her face softened. With a nervous glance to Rinnah, she continued. "And maybe so you can understand why I would like to become good friends with your father."

Rinnah looked at Meagen and found her returning Sandy's gaze with a look of shame.

"And I also wanted to tell you that I am a grown woman who has worked very, very hard to get where I am. I may not yet deserve *your* friendship, but I do deserve your respect and a few good manners."

Meagen blushed and looked away.

"Don't ever treat me the way you did at lunch today, Meagen. It was appalling and embarrassing to your father, and I won't stand for it. I don't have to."

Then Sandy Price left, without saying another word.

FRIENDS 4 EVER?

CHAPTER TWENTY

DINNER THAT NIGHT was miserable.

Meagen tried to hide in her room, but Mr. Paige refused to allow it. So instead, she sat sulking and picking at her food as Mrs. Lane tried in vain to make lighthearted conversation.

"I hear the grand finale of the Mt. Rushmore fireworks is the longest in the country," she said.

"Really?" Mr. Paige asked. Mrs. Lane gave an "Oh, yes" as she spooned more spaghetti sauce on Tommy's mound of pasta.

"I can't wait to see that," Mr. Paige said.

Rinnah watched as Meagen picked apart her garlic bread. Since Sandy's visit, Meagen had remained sullen and had not uttered more than a couple words all afternoon. But because Rinnah still stung from Meagen's unkind remarks, she hadn't gone out of her way to speak to Meagen, either.

After dinner, neither girl spoke to the other as they helped Mrs. Lane with the clean up. Even Tommy remained quiet, not knowing how to act with both his best friends fighting.

After several hours of awkward attempts at conversation by Mrs. Lane, the entire household finally dragged itself off to their private rooms one by one. When Rinnah crawled into bed, Meagen's lamp was already off. Rinnah's friend kept her back to the room and slept facing the wall.

The next day, the girls found different things to do to occupy their time. Tommy, in an effort to remain neutral, spent his time as evenly as possible between the two girls. He spent the morning riding horses with Rinnah while Meagen read a book and did some online window shopping. In the afternoon, Tommy explored the Canyon with Meagen while Rinnah viewed Ben's documentary, *The Curse of the Royal Ruby* one more time. By evening, he was exhausted and refused to do anything but sit in the living room and practice magic tricks. But after an hour of awkward silence, Tommy felt like he would go crazy if the girls continued to ignore each other.

"Make up already so I don't have to babysit anymore," he said, sounding a grumpy.

Rinnah turned to Meagen, who sat on the sofa trying to watch TV through the snowy reception.

"Hey, Meagen. Let's——"

"I'm gonna check e-mail," Meagen interrupted. She grabbed her laptop and opened the lid without looking up.

Rinnah sighed and went to a corner of the room, where she opened her bag and brought out her notepad to examine clues and do a little fact-checking.

Tommy was the only one who accepted Mrs. Lane's offer of freshly baked chocolate cake when she came in later to help liven things up a little.

"More for me," he said before devouring the first of two pieces.

The next morning, Meagen was already gone when Rinnah got up.

"She's out riding Buck Eye," Mrs. Lane explained when Rinnah asked. She gave Rinnah a pat on her head and said, "She'll come around, Princess. Just give her time."

Rinnah went back to her room and got some clothes and a towel to take a shower and get ready for the day. When she got to the bathroom, she had to clean up the mess Meagen had left behind. As she put away the make-up and dirty clothes, she knew that today would be a rerun of yesterday, with her and Meagen not spending any time together, or even talking. And she really wanted Meagen's help tonight. Of all nights to be fighting with one of her best friends, the night when she could crack the mystery of the Royal Ruby and help track down Lily's killer.

Rinnah wondered if she would ever be able to make things right with Meagen. Turning on the shower, she mumbled to herself as she waited for the water to get hot.

"This is gonna be a totally lousy summer."

THE MAGIC HOUR
CHAPTER TWENTY-ONE

IT WAS NEARLY dusk by the time they reached Mt. Rushmore.

Rinnah bolted from the Jeep, her heart thumping in her chest. Her hands shook as she locked the Jeep's door, and she tried to steady them by clutching the medicine bag that hung around her neck. Beside her, Sandy Price's black BMW sedan came to a halt. Mrs. Lane waved wildly from the passenger side.

"Oh, I just love fireworks!" she said as she hoisted herself out of the car. She slammed her door shut and looked around the parking structure for the nearest exit.

"I hope we're not too late to get some good seats."

"Me, too!" Tommy shouted. His voice echoed within the parking structure and mingled with others as families unloaded from mini vans and SUVs.

"Looks like this is the way to go," Mrs. Lane said, with a wave of a pudgy hand toward an EXIT sign. Mr. Paige and Sandy closed their doors and an electronic chirp sounded as Meagen's dad locked the vehicle.

The group joined the throng of people making their way out of the parking structure and up the stairs. Tommy took the lead and jumped the steps two at a time until they all emerged from the underground lot into the glowing twilight. Rinnah recalled a behind-the-scenes show she watched on TV where movie stars talked about the filmmaking process. Looking at the sky, she knew that they called this the "magic hour," when light from the waning sun gave up its brightness in purple hues just before night fell. Movie scenes shot during this time developed with a special beauty and were reserved for the most important aspects of the storytelling. If Ben knew how close Rinnah was to finding the Rose, would he be here now, with his camera, to document the moment with a moviemaker's eye? Rinnah shuddered and silently scolded herself for such a dramatic train of thought.

"Geeky much?" she muttered to herself as she followed

her friends away from the parking structure. She looked around and hoped her suspicions were correct. Sage, the writer of the mysterious note, should be here. And Rinnah had a lot of questions that needed answers.

Rinnah walked farther down a wide lane lined with the flags from each of the 50 states—the Avenue of the Flags. As her eyes followed the flags, they came to rest on a mountain where four faces were carved into the granite. Brilliant lights illuminated Washington, Lincoln, Roosevelt, and Jefferson as they stared with an unblinking gaze, their likenesses forever frozen in time.

"Take care under their stony gaze..."

Rinnah shivered as she remembered the note, the coded message that Sage wrote to Lily. A note describing the when and where of their secret meeting. For what? To hand off the rose? The crown jewel of a dethroned queen? She hoped she was right, but found herself afraid in spite of it.

Rinnah had been to Mt. Rushmore many times before, but could never believe how unreal the faces looked, like one of the many picture postcards sold in gift shops all over South Dakota. She learned early on that it took over 14 years to make, its creator stopping only because of his death in 1941.

Tourists stopped to take pictures and point with ice-cream-dripping fingers. Rinnah had to dodge the backs of more than a few as they screeched to a halt every few steps, trying to catch a new angle before the light faded completely.

Over the PA system, Rinnah listened as the music from the lighting ceremony came to a close. An announcement was made that the fireworks show would be starting shortly.

"Let's get a move on!" Tommy shouted over the din of the crowd. He skipped ahead, bobbing and weaving through the crowd like a rookie football player. Mr. Paige clasped Sandy's hand and picked up the pace. Mrs. Lane jostled forward, parting the crowd for Meagen to follow with a minimum of toe stepping. Rinnah hurried forward as well, her heart pounding with each step she took. Once again, she clasped the medicine bag in her sweaty palm.

When she reached the outdoor amphitheater, Rinnah saw that Tommy had saved a row of seats by laying across them. Mr. Paige chuckled at the sight.

"Sit up, squirt, and relinquish a few of those seats," he said with a good-natured pat on the boy's shoulder.

Rinnah looked up in time to see Tommy scowl as he got up and made room for the adults. As he took a seat at the end of the row, Rinnah leaned over.

"He didn't mean anything by it, Tommy," she whispered.

Tommy tried to act casual as he asked, "Who?"

"Mr. Paige," Rinnah answered. "He didn't mean anything by calling you 'squirt.'"

Tommy blushed and watched as Meagen's dad disentangled himself from Mrs. Lane's scarf.

"I know. I guess…"

Rinnah decided that now was not the time to get into a deep discussion with Tommy about his height, or his unnecessary self-consciousness about it. Instead, she allowed her eyes to fall on her other friend who chose to sit next to Mrs. Lane.

Meagen remained silent, even as those around her struck up friendly conversation with her father and Mrs. Lane. She just squinted under the flood of stadium lighting and avoided the chatter that drew Mrs. Lane in like a Siren's song.

"So, you think she's ever gonna talk to you again?"

Rinnah fiddled with her bag and continued gazing at Meagen. "I don't know, Tommy. But I don't have time to deal with that right now." She opened the bag and began to rummage through its contents.

"Yeah, we have to be on the lookout for Sage," Tommy said in a gush of breath. He stood on his seat and began looking through the crowd with ridiculous intensity.

"Sit down, Tommy!" Rinnah hissed. "You don't even know who you're looking for."

Tommy sat with a scowl and muttered, "Well, neither do you, yeah?"

Rinnah's skin prickled as she thought to herself that Tommy was right. Who was Sage? And how was she going to find him—or her—in the midst of these people? But one thing she did know; she had to at least look, for Lily's sake.

As people took their seats around her, Rinnah pulled a pair of binoculars out from her bag. She put them to her eyes and adjusted them. Finally, she pulled them down and thrust them back into her bag.

"These are no good. It's too dark to see anything."

Indeed, with the sun now behind a nearby mountain, the shadow that fell over the amphitheater was as dark as nighttime. Only the sky overhead remained a deep purple, like that of a fresh bruise.

Rinnah sat back and tried to calm herself. Her mind, however, continued going over Ben's documentary on the Rose. Something still didn't sit right with her, something she couldn't quite determine. Now she was taking the place of a dead woman for a secret meeting. What if the killer knows? Did Lily say anything before the pillow was put over her face, silencing her forever? The seal on the note was broken ... surely she had read it.

Suddenly, the lights dimmed, causing the crowd to applaud wildly.

Rinnah's body shook with fear as she slid from her seat. "Time for the fireworks."

ILLUMINATING DEEDS
CHAPTER TWENTY-TWO

When Rinnah rose from her seat, she had to clamp a hand over Tommy's mouth and shush him before he caught the attention of Mrs. Lane or Meagen's dad. She didn't need the grown-ups to know that she was trying to leave.

"I'll be right back," she lied. "I'm just gonna go to the snack bar."

Rinnah released her hand slowly from Tommy's mouth, but the look on his face told her that he didn't believe her. When Rinnah stood, her gaze fell on Meagen. The girl was watching her. And even though they hadn't spoken in what seemed like forever, Rinnah read the look on her face as well. She was scared, scared for Rinnah.

An explosion ripped through the air, and a sunburst of color lit the sky. In that shining second, Meagen mouthed the words "Be careful." Rinnah smiled and nodded. She threw in an OK sign with her fingers for good measure.

Making sure the grown-ups weren't looking, Rinnah slipped out of the row and walked up the steps to the top landing. When she got there, a crowd of people stood blocking her exit, their eyes lifted to the colorful night sky.

"Excuse me."

No one could hear her over the sounds of fireworks exploding in mid air. Finally, she gently shoved through the mass until she came out the other side. Before her stood a concession stand, currently empty of any customers.

Rinnah continued walking until she found herself back on the Avenue of the Flags. A few people still milled about, but further down the avenue, a lone figure sat on a large boulder. Rinnah cocked her head as she peered down the lane. Something about the way the shoulders slumped seemed oddly familiar. Then the figure stood. A hand went up, beckoning to Rinnah.

Another crash and an explosion of colored light. In the split-second of blindness following the light, a memory came to Rinnah.

"It couldn't be!" she said.

She thought more about the clues and soon found her heart racing with what they suggested.

Rinnah walked further down the asphalt path, squinting in an effort to see between the firework blooms, to see if she was right. To see if Sage was someone she knew. Someone she trusted.

Her heart raced and she found her breath coming in short bursts. With each explosion of fireworks, she was sure her heart would leap out of her chest.

She continued walking, and noticed the figure beside the boulder stir as she grew nearer. Rinnah froze, her scalp tingling with the memory of the fish hatchery and the shadow that stood in the restroom doorway.

Rinnah began to move again, walking faster with each step she took.

"The time has come for our independence..."

Rinnah found herself reciting the note as she walked further down the lane. She talked to calm herself, not realizing fully what she was saying.

"Take great care under their stony gaze—"

She jumped as another explosion of fireworks filled the air. For the first time, she could smell the burning sulfur. The smoke from the dying embers shrouded her, swirling between her legs like a glowing, living fog. She continued walking. And talking.

"—for the exploding heavens shall illuminate our deeds."

Before she knew it, Rinnah stood at the base of the South Dakota flag. Another flash of light and the figure moved, causing the air, thick and acrid with the smoke of fireworks, to swirl away in roiling coils. As the smoke cleared, the figure spoke.

"Did you bring the note with you?"

Rinnah gasped, ignoring the question as she stepped closer to the man beneath the flag. With another burst of fireworks, recognition flared within Rinnah like the brilliant fire that danced in the sky.

"So you are Sage!"

With that, a rough pair of hands grasped Rinnah's shoulders and a familiar face loomed above her as Rinnah said the name of her medicine man.

"Ronnie Black Elk!"

SAGE

CHAPTER TWENTY-THREE

RONNIE BLACK ELK nodded. As he spoke, Rinnah felt the fear melt from her. His voice was familiar, comforting.

"You shouldn't be here, Rinnah," he said.

Rinnah stepped foreword, trying to hear him above the crashing of the fireworks show.

"I know. But I want to help that lady, the poor lady that was killed. Cassandra." Then, softly and almost to herself, "Lily."

Ronnie's hands gave a light squeeze to Rinnah's shoulder.

"I know," he said over the booming light show. "I saw her give you the note back at the fish hatchery and cursed the woman for her foolishness."

"But she was scared. She didn't know what else to do!" Rinnah shouted at Sage, but not just because of the noise. She felt herself growing upset over Lilly's last attempt at saving the Rose—and she didn't want to fail the woman now.

"This is more dangerous than you can possibly imagine, Rinnah," the man said. "There are secrets to protect, secrets that are generations older than you or I."

Rinnah clasped the hand that laid on her shoulder. "But I need to know them. Lily... Cassandra... whoever, she can't die for nothing!"

The night lit up with the colors of fireworks. Red, yellow, and green explosions flared overhead. Their light shifted over the worn, familiar face of Ronnie, the man who called himself Sage.

"The Florist is here," he said.

Rinnah nodded. "Do you know who it is?" she asked.

Ronnie looked around for any suspicious spectators, but the Avenue of the Flags was empty.

"No, I don't. But I have to assume that whoever it is, they know the contents of that note."

As the medicine man looked into Rinnah's eyes, she

could tell that he thought the same thing she did. That the Florist may have gotten Lily to talk before killing her.

As the sky above her boomed with the thunder of the exploding show, Rinnah tried to decide what to do next. Rockets whistled into the sky, followed by yet more explosions. From the corner of her eye, Rinnah noticed curious sparks leap from the boulder behind Ronnie. He spun around in alarm, his face showing an emotion Rinnah had never seen there before. Fear.

Another crack ripped through the smoke-filled night around them, but no explosion of light followed. Rinnah looked around, confused but not knowing why.

Suddenly, it made sense.

"Oh my God!" she cried.

Ronnie grabbed Rinnah by the hand.

"We have to run."

Rinnah's head spun as Ronnie whirled her around, back toward the amphitheater.

"That was a bullet," she whispered. "Someone's shooting at you."

Rinnah heard more explosions as Ronnie pulled her away from the boulder and whispered in her ear.

"It's the Florist."

The sky lit up a dazzling red. Rinnah raised her eyes and saw another large red explosion, the bloom of which seemed to span for miles. Red lights shimmered and danced, making Rinnah swoon with the beauty—and the horror—of it.

"They're like rubies…"

She felt herself being jerked forward.

"Girl, we have to run!"

Rinnah followed Ronnie down the smoky Avenue of the Flags. He tried to run faster, tried to pull Rinnah into the chase, but his body couldn't support his will.

Rinnah felt as if she were in a dream, in a nightmare from which she couldn't wake. The world moved in slow motion around her, flashing first in yellow, then green, then red, as if she were looking through glasses that changed in color with each crashing heartbeat. People all around them, but not seeing. Their eyes were cast heavenward, their minds filled with explosions of light, and color, and sound.

Rinnah rested her hand on a flagpole as Ronnie tried to pull her along. Suddenly, she felt something strike the metal, strike it hard. Even over the crash of fireworks, she heard the ricochet of a bullet.

Rinnah screamed.

"Run!"

Her mind came back to her, the paralyzing spell of fear being broken like the fragile shell of a hollow egg. She tightened her grip on Ronnie's hand and began pulling him along as she tried to run faster.

The whistling of rockets screamed through the night. Five, six, maybe more. Then, the explosions began. A few at first, then building with more and more until the night turned to day. Bright colors filled her vision as Rinnah began to drag Sage behind her.

The grand finale.

Rinnah pulled harder.

"We have to get off the pavement!"

Rinnah heard Ronnie's warning cry and knew what he meant. With all this light, he would make a perfect target.

Rinnah leapt off the path and into the brush that lined the Avenue of the Flags. With Ronnie at her heels, she hopped from one boulder to another, each placed strategically to fulfill the landscape designer's artistic vision. Well-pruned trees were spaced evenly between the rocks, but provided little cover.

Rinnah ducked behind a large boulder with the hope of hiding out until the grand finale completed its spectacle. She peered cautiously to her left, back toward the South Dakota flag. She looked over to Sage when she felt his hand slip from her own.

"Are you OK?"

Ronnie nodded, but his face was pale and beaded with

sweat. Rinnah laid a hand on his forehead and gasped when she felt the coldness of his brow. It was then that she noticed the blood.

"You've been shot!"

Ronnie clutched his shoulder and winced from the pain.

"Lie still while I get some help!"

Ronnie's hand reached out and grasped Rinnah by the elbow.

"Wait!"

Rinnah paused and looked into his eyes.

"I've come to give you a message. You must hear me…"

The color in Ronnie's face had completely drained away. Rinnah laid a hand to his check and shuddered at the lack of warmth. The death-like pallor from his face seemed to glow from within the shadows, causing Rinnah to look around in panic.

"I've got to call someone!"

A spasm of pain rocked Ronnie and both hands went to his shoulder. He hissed between gritted teeth.

"You can't let them find the Rose," he rasped. "You have to…" But that was all that came. With a sigh, Ronnie's head relaxed and rolled to one side.

Rinnah loosened the bandanna from around the medicine man's neck and pulled it free. She wadded it into a ball and forced it into the wound. Ronnie stirred, rocked by another spasm of pain. Rinnah took his hands and forced them to cover the source of the bleeding.

The sound of rockets shrieked from somewhere over Rinnah's shoulder. The crash of explosions and the sky was lit all over again with the colors of the fireworks show.

Rinnah glanced down and noticed something had spilled from Ronnie's grasp. A medicine bag. Larger than her own, but she recognized the shape, the stitching. This one was worn with age, some of the intricate beading having been lost years ago.

She opened the rawhide pouch and felt inside. She stopped breathing, knowing what was inside but pulling it free anyway. She held it up to the final explosions that lit the night sky.

"The Royal Ruby!"

With the fireworks shining through it, the ruby glowed with a blood red intensity that made Rinnah shiver. It was heavy, about half the size of a real rose, but just as beautiful. The carved edges were sharp and sparkled in the light. It looked amazingly life-like, just like a fully-opened rose. Like the rose in Ben's documentary, the one from the Royal gardens.

Rinnah looked at the man that called himself Sage and sucked the smoky air into her lungs. As Ronnie Black Elk laid still in the grass beside her, Rinnah raised her face to the exploding heavens. And began to scream.

THE ROYAL RUBY
CHAPTER TWENTY-FOUR

IT WAS AFTER midnight before Rinnah could stop and collect her thoughts. The police had come and gone. When Ronnie Black Elk had regained consciousness, he remained adamant in his "belief" that the whole thing was an accident—another over-enthusiastic spectator shooting into the sky, like they always do on the 4th of July.

"We Indians can't seem to get away from them gun-toting cowboys."

His granddaughter, Katharine, had been beside herself with worry.

"Grandfather! You are never allowed to leave the reservation again. Look what happens when you do!"

Ronnie had laughed at her, and she laughed back. But her laughter came through tears of fear, and of gratitude, Rinnah thought.

Finally, the paramedics took Ronnie Black Elk to Spearfish General after Sandy used her authority as the hospital's administrator to override their procedures. The local hospital was a good one, but the medicine man wanted to go home. A local doctor declared him stable enough to endure the hour-long ride back to Spearfish, and his wishes were granted.

A news crew was there and had reported on the "accident." Rinnah recognized the reporter from TV, the good-looking Travis Ruff. With the report having already been aired, he was no longer on camera. Rinnah had watched as the reporter preened and strutted like a peacock, snapping orders at the cameraman and being a real jerk. She made a silent vow never to watch his news report again.

Now, Rinnah sat in the back seat of the Jeep with Mrs. Lane holding her close.

"What on earth am I going to tell your mother?" she had asked for about the thousandth time. "She'll run me out on a rail for letting this happen!"

Meagen sat in the front seat, her eyes bulging with excitement. It was all she could do to keep from asking Rinnah what *really* happened.

Tommy rode back with Sandy so that Mrs. Lane could continue to comfort Rinnah on the ride back to the cabin.

"Another reason handguns should be outlawed. Imagine, bringing an actual gun to a place filled with families. And children."

Mrs. Lane was on a rant. Rinnah knew from experience that there was no stopping her when she stepped up on that soap box of hers. Instead, Rinnah wiggled beneath the itchy, wool blanket that Mrs. Lane insisted she stayed covered in. Rinnah was sweating beneath that blanket and the heavy arms of her protector.

"An idiot!" Mrs. Lane went on. "Oh, if I could find that man, I would just—"

Mrs. Lane stopped. Rinnah suspected that she was about to say "shoot him," but, under the current situation, chose not to. Rinnah had tried telling the overprotective woman that she was fine, but Mrs. Lane was hearing none of it.

Rinnah let it go and hugged her bag from beneath the blanket, the Royal Ruby safely hidden inside. At least for the time being. The Florist was obviously aware of the meeting and came to collect the ruby. But now the Florist had to know that Rinnah had it. Despite the warmth of the wool blanket, Rinnah shivered at the thought.

There was also the issue of what to do with the Royal Ruby now that she had it. Lily lost her life trying to retrieve it, but for what purpose? Rinnah chewed at her bottom lip, mulling it over.

And why did Ronnie Black Elk have it? He mentioned secrets that were generations old, obviously connected in some way to the ruby. She knew the jewel was lost when the Queen of Varna escaped her country. Rumor had it that the jewel was in her possession when she fled. How did it end up in South Dakota, in the hands of a medicine man?

Rinnah wondered if she shouldn't take another look at Ben's documentary. There were bound to be more answers there.

She thought of other ways to investigate the mystery, to find out who was responsible for the murder of Lily, and the attempted murder of her medicine man.

After a while, her thoughts began to drift further and further away from the events of the evening. With the gentle rocking of the Jeep and Mrs. Lane's soothing caresses to her forehead, Rinnah soon fell fast asleep.

The sound of a car door slamming jolted Rinnah awake.

She blinked the cobwebs of sleep from her mind and looked around. Mrs. Lane smiled down at her as Rinnah rubbed her eyes.

"We're home, sweetie," she said as she brushed the hair from Rinnah's eyes. "Or back at the cabin, anyway."

Rinnah followed Mrs. Lane from the Jeep and stepped out into the cool night air. She closed the door and turned around just in time to see Ben Forrest follow Mr. Paige into their rented home.

"Ben's here," Rinnah observed.

"Oh, he was here when we drove up," Mrs. Lane explained. "He said he heard about the accident on the 11 o'clock news."

Rinnah quickened her step, eager to get inside and see if she could score some quality chat-time with the young filmmaker.

When she entered the living room, Rinnah found Ben sitting on the sofa, talking to Mr. Paige. As Rinnah expected, Meagen was seated next to him—but a little further down.

Guess she's not that fearless after all, Rinnah thought.

She took a seat on the arm of the sofa, right next to Meagen. Her friend looked up and offered a quick smile. Dying to know how the ride home was, Rinnah asked Meagen, "Where's Sandy?"

Meagen blushed slightly before answering.

"Making coffee."

Tommy came out of the kitchen then, holding several cookies in each hand.

"Want one?" he mumbled through a full mouth. Rinnah and Meagen each took one and began eating in silence.

"...And he's really going to be all right?" Ben was asking Mr. Paige. Meagen's dad nodded.

"Looks that way. He's a very lucky man."

Ben's hands gripped his knees, his fingers occasionally drumming the kneecaps. He fidgeted and shook his head.

"I don't suppose they found the guy?..."

Mr. Paige shook his head and said "Nope."

Ben looked up and saw Rinnah. "So how are *you* holding up?"

Rinnah smiled and shrugged. "I'm cool."

Ben smiled awkwardly and Rinnah noticed how tense he seemed. She finished her cookie and held her hand out for a second one. Tommy tossed her one from the coffee table on which he sat.

"I'll go and fetch us some coffee, Ben," Mr. Paige said as he stood from his chair.

"Thanks, that would be great."

Meagen perked up at the mention of coffee. "I'll take some too," she said. "Cream and sugar?"

Her dad frowned. "No way! You'll never get any sleep tonight."

Meagen slouched into the sofa, pouting and crossing her arms. Now that the adults were preoccupied in the kitchen, Rinnah made her move on Ben.

"I have something to ask you, Ben," she began. He responded by raising his eyebrows, encouraging Rinnah to ask away.

"It's about living in Hollywood."

Ben furrowed his brow. His busy fingers stopped their dancing and hovered above each knee.

"What about it?"

Rinnah knew she must tread very carefully over the topic she was about to bring up. She stood and walked around the coffee table as she spoke.

"Well, I heard about what happened when you were in high school…"

"Uh huh…"

Ben settled back in his seat. His eyes narrowed with the curiosity of where this conversation might be headed. Rinnah sat at the chair that Meagen's dad vacated moments before. She leaned forward and fingered her medicine bag as she spoke.

"Well, I was curious about that woman that drowned in your pool…"

Ben head snapped back as if he were slapped.

"Well, you just get right to the point, don't ya?"

Rinnah glanced at Meagen and found that the girl had pulled the neck of her sweater over her face in embarrassment. Tommy just shook his head and munched another cookie. Rinnah looked back at Ben.

"Sorry," she mumbled.

Ben sighed deeply and let the silence fill the room. Finally, he spoke again.

"It was a very hard time for me, as you can probably imagine," he said. "That woman needed help. She was stalking my dad, trying to get him to make some really lame movie she had written."

Rinnah, having regained some of the composure she lost with her opening, perked up and listened with great interest at every word Ben spoke.

"She broke into the house that day and left a note, a note that my dad paid a lot of money to keep out of the papers."

A rustling noise came from Meagen as she withdrew her face from the purple sweater. Even Tommy had stopped his noisy chewing as Ben continued with his story.

"She said some horrible things about my dad in that note, but that wasn't the worst part of it. In fact, finding her body in the pool when I got home from school that day wasn't even the worst of it."

Rinnah held her breath and waited for him to go on. Finally, he did.

"No, I think the worst part of the whole thing was knowing that some of those horrible things she said in the note were actually true."

Rinnah sat still and let her silence do the talking for her. She couldn't imagine how awful the whole thing must have been, to find a note saying terrible stuff about your dad. And to know that some of it was true.

"So as soon as you finished school, you came here," Meagen said. "To get away from all that."

Ben blinked and shook his head.

"Well, no. Not really," he answered.

Rinnah looked a little shocked. So did Meagen and Tommy. Seeing their puzzled expressions, Ben continued.

"I came here to find the Rose."

Before Rinnah could even gasp, Mr. Paige came in to the room.

"Here's your coffee, Ben."

WICKED DREAMS

CHAPTER TWENTY-FIVE

Rinnah Two Feathers screamed.

"RUN!"

Someone followed her, closing the gap in a furious burst of speed, but Rinnah couldn't quite make out who it was.

With her heart pounding in her chest, Rinnah tried to run faster, but she couldn't. She moved in slow motion. She pumped her legs as hard as she could and felt an icy surge of adrenaline kick into her bloodstream, but it was no use. She couldn't move fast enough.

Something crashed overhead. As she tried to run, Rinnah looked up and saw the sky filled with light the color of blood.

BOOM!

Another crash.

"Fireworks."

She looked behind her, into the dark. Another booming crash sounded and night turned to day. She could see her pursuer as his face flashed beneath the multicolored light of fireworks.

It was Ben Forrest. He grinned like a maniac and screamed. "The stony gaze, Rinnah. Can you see it?"

Rinnah looked up and saw faces carved into a mountain. She blinked and looked again, but instead of seeing the faces of four dead presidents, she saw only the likeness of Ronnie Black Elk carved into the stone.

The sky rumbled with more crashing, loud enough to shake the ground. Rinnah covered her ears with her hands, but the rumbling of the sky was too much. The crashing rattled her to the bone.

Rinnah couldn't run any more. Slowly, she turned around.

"Aaaahhhh!" She screamed again as Ben fell upon her. He grabbed her by the shoulders and yelled. "Give me the Rose!"

Rinnah trembled and lifted a fist. She opened it and discovered the Royal Ruby. She offered it to Ben, her hand shaking violently with fear.

Ben took the ruby and looked at it. His face contorted in rage. He threw the ruby to the ground. With another dangerous step forward, Ben yelled at Rinnah, spittle flying from his mouth with each angry word.

"Give me the Rose!"

The sky flashed a brilliant shade of red. More fireworks launched into the sky and exploded all around her. They crashed and rumbled in a deafening roar.

Rinnah froze as Ben lunged at her again, his eyes wild with the look of madness. His large, callused hands wrapped themselves around her throat and began to squeeze.

Rinnah gasped and sat up in bed. She pulled at her throat and found her tiny medicine bag had wrapped itself around her neck.

Another crash sounded and Rinnah yelped. She looked out the window and saw that it was morning. And it was raining cats and dogs.

"God, what a nightmare!"

She remembered the night before, how Ben had claimed to come to Spearfish Canyon to look for the Rose. Once the grown-ups had entered the room, Rinnah chose not to ask more questions with them around. But she couldn't get alone with him anymore that night. Finally, she had gone to bed, too exhausted to even talk to Meagen and Tommy about getting the Royal Ruby. She merely told them that she did, in fact, have it and that it was safe.

"Good morning!"

Rinnah looked up to see Meagen enter the bedroom. She noticed that she was dressed and that her bed was already made. She also noticed that Meagen had skimped a little on the make-up—just some mascara and lip gloss.

"Morning," Rinnah mumbled. She rubbed her eyes and yawned. Thunder crashed and faded to a growling rumble.

"You feeling OK?," Meagen asked. She sat on her own bed and looked at Rinnah with some concern. "You look a little not-yourselfy."

Rinnah nodded.

"Wicked dreams. And not the cool kind."

Meagen gave a quick nod, but remained silent. She looked about the room, suddenly becoming uncomfortable. So did Rinnah. And she didn't like it. Meagen was her best friend, and she missed her, even if had been only two days since they spoke.

The silence seemed to last forever. Finally, Rinnah couldn't stand it anymore. She started talking.

"Meagen, I didn't mean——"

"Rinnah, I'm so sorry."

Meagen stared at her hands as they twisted the bottom of her sweater. She looked up with a sadness in her eyes that made Rinnah's heart ache.

"Seeing my dad with Sandy made me so angry. At first I didn't really understand why, so I just got kinda ... obnoxious, I guess. And when you called me on it, it just made me angrier."

Rinnah shook her head.

"I know, Meagen. I'm sorry. It was so wrong of me to get in your face about it."

Meagen looked down at her hands again. Rinnah noticed that she worked at tying a knot where the yarn had come loose from the hem of her sweater.

"I'm just afraid."

"Afraid of what?" Rinnah asked.

"Afraid of liking her."

Then it became clear to Rinnah just what Meagen had been dealing with.

"And you're afraid that if you do like her, then she'll leave you," Rinnah said softly. "Like your mom did."

Meagen's face turned red and tears shone in her eyes. Her voice quavered as she spoke again.

"I called her yesterday. My mom."

Rinnah pulled the covers back and sat on the edge of her bed, her heart aching at the pain Meagen felt. But she stayed quiet and let Meagen talk.

"Some guy answered. When I said who I was, he covered the phone and I heard him mumble to someone. Then he got back on and said she wasn't there."

Rinnah went and sat next to Meagen. She put her hand on Meagen's back and felt a sob break.

"She wouldn't talk to me. I know she was there, but she wouldn't talk to me."

As the sobs took her, Rinnah put her arms around Meagen. She rocked her slowly as Meagen cried. Rinnah knew the loss that Meagen felt, and began to cry with the memory of her own pain, the kind of pain her best friend was feeling now. They cried together, holding each other tight until the tears stopped coming. Meagen broke away and wiped her face.

"You know something?" Meagen asked when she caught her breath. "This whole thing would be a lot easier if Sandy wasn't so nice."

Rinnah laughed.

"Yeah. The nerve of some people."

Just then, Tommy bounded into the room.

"It's about time you're up," he said. He plopped heavily on the bed beside Rinnah. Then he noticed the girls' puffy faces. His eyes narrowed suspiciously.

"Have you guys been crying?"

Rinnah punched Tommy in the arm.

"Ow! What was that for?"

Rinnah stood from the bed and dropped back onto her own.

"For being an insensitive geek-boy."

"Well, at least you guys have made up, yeah?"

"Yeah," Meagen said. "It's all good."

"OK, then. Moving on," Tommy said. He cast Rinnah an expectant look.

"What?" she asked.

Tommy sighed, his patience having run out hours ago.

"Hello!" Tommy said as he grabbed Rinnah's ankle. "Let's see the ruby, yeah?"

Meagen perked up, her eyes going wide with the mention of the ruby.

Rinnah pulled her bag out from under the covers.

"I slept with it last night, just to be safe."

She rummaged through the backpack and found the large medicine bag. She removed it and examined the beadwork, noticing the design for the first time.

"A rose, of course," she said and showed it to her friends. A lot of the beads were now missing, but the design was clearly visible.

Rinnah opened the bag and pulled out the ruby. Meagen

and Tommy gasped. Even in the darkened bedroom, the ruby glowed brightly. It was as if a fire was burning inside, making it glow with a strange luminescence.

"Wow!" Meagen cried.

"That's gotta be worth a million bucks, yeah?"

Rinnah stood and held the ruby out to Tommy. He shrunk back, his eyes wide with fright.

"I'm not touching that thing. It's cursed!"

Meagen snorted and took the ruby from Rinnah.

"Gosh. It's heavy."

She held it up and examined it against the white background of the bedroom's ceiling.

"And gorgeous," she said.

As Meagen continued gazing at the ruby, Rinnah remembered her dream. In her mind, she saw the way Ben looked as he chased her for the Ruby. How he demanded the rose, only to throw it away in anger.

"Rinnah."

Rinnah snapped back to reality and found Meagen holding the ruby toward her. She took it and put it back in the beaded medicine bag.

"What are you gonna do with it?" Tommy asked.

Rinnah put the medicine bag back into her backpack. "I don't know yet. I'll figure that out later."

As Rinnah pulled the drawstrings of her bag closed, Meagen sat beside her on the bed.

"So, tell us what happened last night," Meagen said.

As Rinnah began recounting the events of the previous night, Tommy crossed his legs and sat on the floor in front of the bed. He didn't say a word until Rinnah had finished.

"But, how did you know it was Ronnie?" he asked.

"Well," Rinnah answered. "It kind of came to me when I remembered this." With that, Rinnah held up her own medicine bag. "He put rose petals in it. Not your typical medicine bag ingredient. Of course, I didn't know for sure, but then I saw him under the South Dakota flag at Mt. Rushmore. He was waiting for me, 'cause he saw Lily give me the note the day of the race. That was him, standing in the doorway of the restroom."

After providing a few more details, Rinnah laid a hand over her growling stomach.

"What's for breakfast?" she asked. "I'm starving."

Tommy jumped from the floor, the thought of food replacing his interest in Rinnah's story.

"Let's find out."

Meagen sighed and rolled her eyes.

"Guess it's time to eat," she said. "If you remember anything you've left out, you have to tell us."

Rinnah said she would and got out of bed. Even now that she was fully awake, she couldn't shake the feeling the dream had left in her. A feeling like it was trying to tell her something.

Rinnah left the room, talking to herself as she did so.

"The Rose. Give me the Rose."

INDIAN BLOOD

CHAPTER TWENTY-SIX

BELLY BLOATED WITH too many pancakes, Rinnah sat in the living room and watched rain streak the windows. The thunder and lightning had stopped, leaving only a dreary drizzle that promised to last throughout the day.

Meagen sat cross-legged on the floor, surfing the net on her laptop.

"I'm doing more research into the Royal Ruby," she had explained.

Rinnah gave her friend a sly wink and watched as Mrs. Lane dusted rental cabin knick-knacks that sat in random groupings on a small table. Tommy sat in front of the coffee table and reviewed his magician's tools: A paper cone made from a newspaper, an empty pickle jar, a juice glass, a black wand, a large square of red velvet, a carton of milk, and his magician's handbook, which he referred to often and with great concentration.

Meagen's dad had gone to work hours ago and hinted that he might be working late.

"That's why I'm here," Mrs. Lane had said. "Don't even worry about things at home. I've got it all under control."

Now the woman set upon the house with a vengeance, cleaning as if the slightest smudge on a windowpane was a personal insult. She even dressed for the occasion in a bright yellow terrycloth tracksuit covered with a huge apron. The large, yellow flowers made Rinnah guess that the apron had started out life as a vintage table cloth. Pristine white tennis shoes with pink pom-poms bouncing from her heels completed Mrs. Lane's cleaning ensemble.

A knock came from the front door. Mrs. Lane froze in mid-swipe and looked to the kids with a horrified expression.

"Whoever could that be?" She whispered so loud that Rinnah was sure that whoever it was had heard the woman.

Mrs. Lane ran to a mirror and patted her hair. With a

quick smoothing of her apron, she went to the door and pulled it open.

"Hey, guys!"

Ben walked in and wiped his feet on the old towel Mrs. Lane put out when it started raining. He smiled and waved as he entered the room.

Just as Mrs. Lane was about to close the door, Victor Little Horn walked in. He scowled when Tommy rolled his eyes.

Mrs. Lane ushered them into the room with a bright smile and a warm offer.

"Can I get you boys something hot to drink? Cocoa, maybe?"

Victor gave an obnoxious snort, but Mrs. Lane didn't catch it.

"How about some coffee?" Ben asked. Mrs. Lane nodded and scurried into kitchen, the hostess on a mission.

"So what's up?" Meagen asked as she closed her laptop.

Victor stayed standing, but dropped his backpack next to an empty armchair. After a brief glance to make sure Victor wasn't going to sit, Ben took the chair for himself.

"Just stopping by to make sure things were good here," he said. "There's gonna be more thunderstorms tonight, and I wanted to make sure you guys had everything you needed in case the power goes out."

Tommy, still glaring at Victor, asked, "Why aren't you at work?"

Victor ran a hand through his damp hair and sneered at Tommy.

"Ever try to drive a nail through a soggy two-by-four in the pouring rain, Shortie?"

Tommy blushed and looked away from the older, and bigger, boy.

"Didn't think so."

Ben ignored the exchange and went on.

"Anyway. There should still be some oil lamps and candles in the pantry."

Mrs. Lane came in with two steaming mugs of coffee.

"Yes, I saw those, Ben. They should work just fine." She held out the coffee to Ben and Victor. "It's black. I've got sugar, but I seem to have run out of milk..."

"No, black's fine. Thanks," Ben answered.

Mrs. Lane arched a penciled eyebrow in Victor's direction.

"I'm cool. Thanks, though."

Victor smiled at Mrs. Lane as he took his cup of coffee. Rinnah shook her head when she saw how charming Victor looked when he smiled. He didn't seem to do that very often, and again Rinnah felt sorry for Victor. Life on the reservation had been cruel to him.

Ben cocked his head toward the direction of the coffee table.

"So, you're learning some magic, eh Tommy?"

At the mention of his latest hobby, Tommy's face brightened, and he began pointing out the different tricks he was learning from the magic book.

As Tommy performed for his captive audience, Rinnah let her mind wander. She thought more about the dream, watching Ben as he sipped coffee and listened to Tommy. She remembered fireworks and the way Ben threw the Royal Ruby in anger. She also remembered the look on his face as he started to strangle her.

God, what a nightmare.

She thought again about Ronnie Black Elk and remembered how he gave up the ruby, but not yet any of the secrets attached to it. She clutched her own medicine bag, the one he made for her, as she remembered him lying in the grass, bleeding. She tried to shake the image of his blood from her mind. The blood of a medicine man. The blood of an Indian.

Indian blood.

Rinnah sat forward in her chair.

What was it he said about Indian blood?

Tommy's voice droned on in the background. Rinnah's unfocused eyes took in his latest trick while her mind tried putting puzzle pieces together. Tommy waved his wand over the paper cone as it sat in the pickle jar. With his other hand, he poured milk from the carton into the cone.

"There's my milk," Rinnah heard Mrs. Lane saying.

Tommy waved his wand in dramatic flourishes.

"The trick is to keep everyone watching the wand. What they don't see is that I'm really pouring the milk into this little glass *behind* the cone."

Rinnah's heart began to pound as her mind worked with the final piece of the puzzle. All the while, she watched Tommy perform his magic trick.

"Keep your audience focused on something else," Tommy was saying. "So they don't see what's going on behind the scenes."

Rinnah gasped.

"That's it!"

She jumped from her chair.

"What?!" Mrs. Lane had jumped from hers, startled at Rinnah's outburst.

"How could I have been so stupid?" Rinnah began to pace, her heart pounding and her pulse racing. "I've had it all wrong. How STUPID!"

Mrs. Lane looked alarmed. "Rinnah, honey? I think you should sit back down. You're working yourself up into a state."

Rinnah ignored her and paced. She mumbled things to herself, things that sounded like gibberish to her group of friends as they watched her with worried expressions.

"Indian blood. The Royal Ruby. The Rose."

Suddenly, she froze. Another thought struck her, one that made her gasp in terror.

"Lily's fortune telling booth!"

Rinnah stepped toward Meagen with a look of anguish.

"We have to go see Ronnie Black Elk!" she blurted.

Mrs. Lane stepped forward. "Princess! You really must calm yourself."

"No! You don't understand. We have to go see him RIGHT NOW!"

Meagen stood and put an arm around Rinnah. "Mrs. Lane's right, Rinnah. Calm down and tell us why."

Suddenly Rinnah felt like a prisoner in the cabin. She had to get out. Had to see Ronnie Black Elk.

"Why do we need to see Ronnie?" Tommy asked.

Rinnah looked around the room and saw the looks of shock that painted her friends' faces. Mrs. Lane. Meagen. Tommy. Ben. Even Victor. Rinnah looked each of them in the eye.

"Because I think I know what it all means!"

KILLING TIME

CHAPTER TWENTY-SEVEN

VICTOR LITTLE HORN smirked as Rinnah paced the room.

"She's totally lost it. I knew it would happen one day."

Ben shushed him into silence.

"We can't see him until visiting hours," Meagen explained. She was doing her best to calm Rinnah down. "That's not 'til eight tonight."

"But there's Sandy," Rinnah said. "She's the administrator. She can get us in to see him now."

Meagen finally lost her patience with Rinnah.

"Rinnah, the poor man has been shot," she yelled. "He needs his rest."

Rinnah stopped and looked at her friend. She sighed and said, "Yeah, you're right. I'm sorry. I guess I'm just getting ahead of myself."

She sat down. "I need to think this through, anyway."

Ben set his coffee mug on the table and stood. "I think maybe we should be taking off."

Victor faked a hurt look. "But we just got here…"

Ben frowned at the remark and made for the door.

"I guess it is time to go," Victor said. He followed his buddy to the door and then turned around. "Uh, thanks for the coffee."

Victor handed his cup to Mrs. Lane while Ben opened the front door.

"Let me know if you need anything," Ben said. He looked at Rinnah as he said it, but it was Mrs. Lane who answered.

"Yes, of course we will, Ben. Stay dry."

After Mrs. Lane waved at them from the front porch, she returned to the living room and sat down in the chair Ben had used while visiting.

"Rinnah, you are so creeping me out right now," Tommy blurted. Rinnah only sighed and stared at his magic supplies. She felt the burn of Mrs. Lane's gaze and turned.

Something caught the corner of her eye when she did so.

"Oh!" she said. "Victor forgot his bag."

Rinnah jumped from the sofa and snatched the bag. By the time she reached the front door and opened it, she saw that Ben's truck was long gone.

"Oh, well. I'm sure he'll come back for it."

"Probably not," Tommy remarked. "He's bound to be too scared to come near this place after your wig-out." Then he smiled. "But that's a good thing, yeah?"

Rinnah closed the front door and hefted the bag back to the sofa. She tossed it to the floor, where it landed with a thud.

"Heavy," she said.

Rinnah sat on the sofa and began to go over the events of the last few days. After a while, she realized how quiet her friends were—especially Mrs. Lane. She looked up and saw everyone staring at her.

"I'm cool," she said. "Really."

Mrs. Lane pursed her orange lips.

"It was a totally random wig, I swear."

Mrs. Lane looked unsure. "But Princess, you said something about a rose," she said with a good deal of concern. "It's just so … random. It makes no sense, whatsoever!"

Rinnah didn't know how to answer the woman, mainly because she didn't want to. She needed to keep what she knew to herself for just a little bit longer. The time would be right later, after she was sure the Rose was safe.

"Uh, I'm just worried about Ronnie, that's all."

Mrs. Lane stared for a few minutes before rising from her chair and making her way out of the room. From the kitchen, Rinnah could hear the sound of water running from the tap and the clinking of dirty coffee cups.

Later that afternoon, it was all Rinnah could do to keep from bolting from the cabin and run screaming all the way down the highway and into Spearfish.

"I've got to talk to Ronnie Black Elk," she kept saying. "Until then, I'm just killing time."

Tommy was tired of hearing it.

"We know already. Change the channel, will ya?"

Meagen rose from her position on the floor and stretched her aching muscles.

"I haven't been able to find out anything more about the Royal Ruby," she said as she rubbed her calves. Rinnah started pacing again, trying to talk things out without giving too much away.

"I've got to come up with a plan to get the Rose to a safe place. And away from the Florist."

Tommy looked up from his magic book and said, "Well I'm not wearing no dress this time."

Meagen chuckled and dropped herself to the sofa. She was about to say something to Tommy, but Rinnah got to him first.

"Does Mr. Lee still organize the booths for Wild West Days?" Rinnah asked.

Tommy shrugged. "Ask your grandmother," he said. "She and her Rez cronies always rent one to sell their frybread."

Meagen frowned at Tommy's description of Grandma Two Feathers's friends.

"You're right," Rinnah said. "I'm gonna make a few phone calls. I have to find out something about Lily's booth at the Wild West Days."

Meagen looked puzzled. "What good will that do?"

Rinnah didn't even stop when she said, "Because I think I know who murdered Lily."

THE MEDICINE MAN

CHAPTER TWENTY-EIGHT

RINNAH STEPPED OUT of Mrs. Lane's Cadillac.

"Finally!" she breathed. She checked her watch. "Five minutes 'til eight."

Meagen and Tommy jumped from the car and waited for Mrs. Lane to lock the doors. When she finished, the kids raced toward the emergency room entrance.

"Wait for me," Mrs. Lane called after them. "And no running in the hallways."

Once Rinnah slipped through the revolving doors, she broke Mrs. Lane's rule. Within minutes, she was in Ronnie Black Elk's room.

"Rinnah!"

Ronnie's granddaughter Katharine greeted Rinnah warmly as she entered the clean, white room. Rinnah smelled the lingering odor of disinfectant and meatloaf. She noticed a dinner tray with half-eaten food sitting on an empty table on wheels.

"It's so nice of you to come and visit Grandfather. You know, he's been asking for you."

"I figured as much," Rinnah nodded. "But we couldn't come 'til the evening visiting hour."

Katharine nodded and led Rinnah to her grandfather. As she stepped up to the metal railing that boxed in the bed, Rinnah heard Meagen and Tommy enter the room.

"Hey, Ronnie," Rinnah greeted. "How are you feeling?"

"Better, now that I know you are safe," the medicine man grunted. "For now."

Rinnah smiled and bent her head low so she could whisper. "It's not my safety you should be worried about, right?"

Ronnie Black Elk closed his eyes and sighed.

"You know too much, girl," he croaked. Then he opened his sleepy eyes and fixed them on Rinnah.

"Are you wearing the medicine bag I blessed for you?"

Rinnah pulled it out from her fleece sweatshirt and showed him.

"Good," he said. "That's good."

A low rumbling filled the silence of the hospital room. Rinnah recognized the sound of thunder coming from miles away. The medicine man stirred.

"A storm is coming."

Rinnah nodded.

"It's going to be a big one," he said.

Rinnah looked at the small window on the far wall. It lit up briefly. Rinnah counted to nine and again heard the low growl of thunder.

"I know about the Rose," Rinnah said. She expected Ronnie to become alarmed, angry, happy, something. Instead he just sighed.

"It is a secret my family has kept for many, many years, Rinnah." He licked his dry, cracked lips and put a finger to his mouth. Rinnah took a plastic cup with a straw in it from the bedside table and put it to the medicine man's lips. He sipped and then waved the glass away.

Rinnah spoke again when his eyes pleaded with her.

"That's why I'm here. To find out what I can do to make sure that the Rose is safe."

The medicine man groaned as he tried to sit up. Growing faint with the effort, he allowed his fevered head to fall back against the pillow. He waited for his breath to come back to him, and then he spoke.

"There is one thing you can do, Rinnah. One thing you *must* do."

Rinnah took the old man's hand in her own and waited. She watched as the smoky coals of fear began to smolder in his eyes. When he spoke again, it was if those embers were burning a hole deep into her soul.

"You must leave the Canyon."

Rinnah gasped. She wasn't sure if she had heard him correctly. "Leave the Canyon?" she repeated. "But why? I need to be here to keep the Rose safe. I need you to tell me how."

Ronnie Black Elk shook his head. "By leaving," he croaked. "That's why I came to you, last night at the fireworks show. To tell you that you must put the Rose out of your mind and leave here. The Florist knows about the Rose ... and about you."

Then, the medicine man looked out the window. "The rain tells me so," he said, his voice barely a whisper.

Rinnah looked confused, but remained silent as the medicine man turned his weary gaze back to her.

"The rain is no longer your friend, Rinnah. It will betray you, like they have betrayed the Rose."

Rinnah shook her head, unable, or unwilling, to accept what Ronnie was telling her.

"But I need to keep the Rose close—"

"No!"

Rinnah jumped.

"You must leave without the Rose. Put the distance of the prairie between you, or you will both be destroyed."

Rinnah lingered beside the hospital bed, not sure what she should do. Raising her head away from the railing, she allowed her eyes to fall upon the monitors and equipment that helped the medicine man to heal, to stay alive.

Ronnie, as if sensing Rinnah's thoughts, looked at the tubes hooked up to his arms and nodded.

"My own medicine can't help me this night," he said. "But perhaps it can help you." With that, he reached out an old, gnarled finger and tapped the medicine bag that swung freely from Rinnah's neck.

Rinnah looked doubtful, even when she said, "I hope so."

THE TROUBLE WITH CADILLACS
CHAPTER TWENTY-NINE

THE RAIN CAME down in buckets as Rinnah, Tommy, Meagen, and Mrs. Lane headed back to the car. But the torrent of rain didn't dampen the resolve Rinnah found on her walk through the hospital. She knew what she must do. As soon as she got back to the cabin, she would call Ben Forrest.

They had stayed only 30 minutes, until Ronnie Black Elk had fallen asleep.

"A good night's rest will do the poor man some good," Mrs. Lane had declared before ushering the kids out of the room.

Now Rinnah climbed into the back seat of the Cadillac and buckled up. Her friends did the same as Mrs. Lane stuck the key in the ignition and turned.

The car wouldn't start.

Mrs. Lane tried again, pumping the gas pedal furiously.

"My word!" she said. "What a night for this to happen."

As Mrs. Lane continued trying to start the car, Rinnah began to get a sinking feeling in the pit of her gut.

"This isn't a coincidence," she said to herself.

Rinnah shivered and became frightened. She clasped the medicine bag and held her breath.

"Come on," she said. "Start!"

But the car whined until they couldn't even hear the sickly sound of the engine trying to turn over. Mrs. Lane seemed insulted at the lack of cooperation from her car.

"Well I never!"

Suddenly someone pounded on Mrs. Lane's window.

"Oh!"

Rinnah could just make out the outline of a hooded figure standing just outside the car. Because the power windows wouldn't work, Mrs. Lane made a move to open the door.

"Wait!"

Everyone in the car turned and looked at Rinnah. By the looks on their faces, she obviously startled them when she cried out.

"Be careful," she said.

Mrs. Lane clucked her tongue and opened the door.

"My goodness. It's Katharine."

"It looks like you're having car trouble."

Mrs. Lane harrumphed in agreement.

"Blasted thing!" she said with a smack to the steering wheel.

"Why don't I give you guys a lift."

Mrs. Lane clapped her hands in delight.

"Aren't you a dear," she said. "That would be heaven."

Rinnah squirmed in her seat.

"No!"

Mrs. Lane looked shocked.

"Whyever not, Rinnah?"

Katharine wiped the rain from her face and peered into the car.

This isn't right, Rinnah thought to herself.

"Uh, um," she stammered. "'Cause you should stay with your grandfather."

Mrs. Lane gave Katharine a look that said she agreed with Rinnah.

"It's OK. He's sleeping now." Katharine said. "I'll come back to check on him after I get you home."

Mrs. Lane seemed to be satisfied with that and got out of the car. Tommy and Meagen did the same and followed

Mrs. Lane as Katharine led them to the next row of the parking lot. Rinnah had no choice to but to go along as well. When Katharine stopped in front of her car, Mrs. Lane took a step back.

"Is this your car?" she asked.

Katharine answered by clicking her remote. The lights of a neon green Volkswagen Beetle blinked on.

"Sweetheart, I have earrings bigger than that."

Tommy laughed and was soon joined by Mrs. Lane.

After catching her breath, Mrs. Lane said, "Why don't you take the kids home, and I'll call a tow truck."

"Well, sure," Katharine said. "But only if you promise to wait in the cafeteria. I'd hate for you to catch cold."

Mrs. Lane promised that she would, and the kids climbed into the Bug. She waved as Rinnah and her friends left the hospital.

During the short ride back to the cabin, Rinnah couldn't shake the feeling that something was wrong. She didn't like the way the Cadillac died, didn't like it at all. And she did not like the fact that Katharine was leaving her grandfather. But Rinnah also wanted to be back in the safety of the cabin, no matter how she got there. She kept looking behind her to see if anyone followed. So far, no one had.

They pulled into the gravel drive leading to the cabin, and Rinnah felt a sense of dread. As lightning tore through the night sky, it illuminated the cabin in bright flashes of light. The strobe effect made it look eerie somehow. As the thunderstorm raged around it, the house suddenly looked evil. Rinnah decided that she didn't want to go in there. It made her skin crawl.

"We're here," Katharine said as she parked the car. Tommy threw open his door, causing the shrieking wind and thunder to fill the car.

"Maybe I should stay with you until Mrs. Lane gets back..." Katharine suggested. When no one appeared to hear her, she shut off the engine and opened her door. Just then, the heavens let loose with another downpour that caught them all off guard.

"Whoa!" Tommy yelled over sound of the storm. "We're about to get very wet."

Rinnah held the car door open for Meagen. As she did so, she swept the house with her eyes. She found her bedroom window right away and stared at it.

"Did I leave the bedroom light on?"

Meagen didn't hear her and was halfway to the front door by the time Rinnah could ask again. She lingered by the car door and watched the glow of her bedroom window.

A shadow passed behind the curtain.

Rinnah gasped.

"Someone's in my room!"

Rinnah took a tentative step away from the car.

The bedroom light went out.

Rinnah began to run toward the house, screaming as she went.

"Don't go in there!" she cried. But the storm was too loud. She watched in horror as Katharine, Tommy, and Meagen walked into the cabin.

Rinnah screamed again. "Get out of the house! Get out!"

Rinnah slipped in the mud just as she reached the front porch. A sob of fear broke her voice as she continued screaming.

"IT'S THE FLORIST!"

THE FLORIST
CHAPTER THIRTY

AFTER SEVERAL FRANTIC tries, Rinnah finally got to her feet. She flung herself onto the wooden porch and through the open door.

"Get out of the house!"

Katharine, Meagen, and Tommy gaped at Rinnah as she flew into the room. Mud and rainwater splashed around her.

No one moved.

Rinnah ran to the phone. She picked up the receiver, but it slipped from her wet hands.

"Nooooo."

She went to her knees and reached under the coffee table. "Where is it?!"

Finally, her hand griped the cordless phone. She snatched it tight and stood, glancing toward her bedroom. In the gloom of the hallway, she could just see that her door was closed.

Thunder crashed, then began to rumble with a deep growl.

Rinnah smeared mud from the face of the phone and pushed the button.

Nothing happened.

She pushed the button again and brought the phone to her ear.

The line was dead.

Rinnah looked toward her bedroom. Fear made her mind swirl with the dreadful images of Lily floating in the fish hatchery and Ronnie Black Elk bleeding as the faces of Mt. Rushmore looked on. Her body shook as she let the phone slip from her wet fingers.

As her friends stared at her in shock, Rinnah looked around the cabin. The only light in the house blazed from the kitchen.

She looked back toward her bedroom door. It remained closed.

"We've got to get out of here," she whispered. "They're after the Rose."

Just as Rinnah ran toward Katharine, the remaining light went out. The room was engulfed in darkness.

Meagen screamed.

"It's the storm," Katharine said. But her voice wavered.

"It's not the storm," Rinnah whispered. "It's the Florist."

Lightning lit the house with a brief flash, and Rinnah moaned with fear at what she saw in that split second.

Her bedroom door was open.

"Quick!" Rinnah whispered. "Get to the loft."

Lightning flashed again and Rinnah saw the terrified looks on the faces of her friends. They stood frozen, paralyzed with fear.

"Move!"

Meagen was the first to snap out of it. Tommy followed, and then Katharine.

Meagen got to the door that led to the stairway. She twisted the handle but nothing happened.

"It won't open!"

Rinnah could hear that Meagen was on the verge of tears.

Lightning flashed again, and Rinnah saw Tommy shove Meagen aside.

"You're pushing it," he said in the blackness that followed. "You need to pull it open."

With that, Rinnah heard the door swing open.

Footfalls sounded with dull thuds as the group ran up the carpeted stairway.

Rinnah jumped in behind them and swung the door closed. Before it slammed, Rinnah stopped and quietly clicked the knob into place.

Rinnah slipped up the stairs and into the loft.

"Keep down," she hissed when she saw Tommy standing at the edge. He obeyed and dropped just below the short wall that overlooked the living room from above.

Katharine and Meagen crouched on either side of Tommy. Rinnah took her place next to them with Meagen just to her left. She held her breath and watched.

Lightning flashed, revealing that the room below was empty.

Thunder exploded, drowning out the sound of the rain as it hit the roof. Windows rattled with the strength of it.

Rinnah peered into the darkness below, willing the shadows to move.

The thunder rumbled away. Rinnah wiped mud from her face. Her hair was soaked and dripped onto the ledge of the loft.

Another flash of lightning. This time, Rinnah gasped. A hooded figure stood in front of the sofa.

Rinnah felt Meagen grip her arm in terror. More thunder shook the house.

The house was dark again. Pitch black.

Rinnah leaned forward, her head hanging dangerously over the loft wall.

A flash of lightning. A snapshot of the figure near the front door. Its rain slicker glistened in the light. Then the darkness.

More thunder crashed. So loud that Rinnah thought the windows would explode with it.

Rinnah edged further out over the loft.

Lightning.

The front door was closed, and the figure had moved. It now stood behind the sofa, directly beneath Rinnah and her friends as they hid in the loft.

The thunder came immediately. Meagen yelped at the strength of it. As Rinnah turned to silence Meagen, her sodden hair swiped across the top of the loft wall. She felt the edge and found puddles of rainwater. Some of it ran down and dripped from the loft.

She turned and looked down.

Lightning lit the room beneath Rinnah.

The figure was looking up at the loft.

Darkness.

Rinnah tried wiping away the rainwater, but it was too late.

The Florist knew where they were.

Thunder again. So loud Rinnah's body shook.

More lightning, this time the thunder came with it. It seemed to last forever. Long enough for Rinnah to see something that made her whine with fear.

A knife.

The figure held it out, point up, like a candle meant to light the darkness of the room. The blade was sharp, clean, jagged at the tip. And it was big.

Rinnah clasped her hand on Meagen's mouth to silence the scream she knew was building.

Before the thunder died, another bolt of lighting lit the room. More thunder pounded against the cabin windows

The figure still held up the knife, tilting it from side to side as if teasing Rinnah with a taste of what was about to come.

Rinnah saw something else, something that confirmed her suspicions.

She saw the figure's hand as it held the knife in a white-knuckled grip.

The hand with the henna tattoo.

The hand of Tina Treadwell.

THE ROSE

CHAPTER THIRTY-ONE

"RINNAH!"

Tina yelled from the darkness below. Rinnah heard her as the thunder faded.

"Give me the Rose!"

Rinnah stayed behind the loft wall, crouching low and shivering.

"I promise I won't hurt you," Tina yelled.

Rinnah thought about Lily, how Tina killed her with a pillow as the woman laid helpless in a hospital bed. She thought about Ronnie Black Elk, Katharine's father, and how Tina shot him, using the fireworks show for cover.

Tina said she wouldn't hurt her. Rinnah didn't believe it for a second.

"Give it to her," Meagen whispered.

Rinnah stayed still.

"Rinnah!" Tommy whined. "Give her the ruby!"

Rinnah shook her head. "No."

Katharine spoke up.

"I don't know what's going on here, Rinnah," she said. "But give that psycho whatever she wants."

Meagen nodded with a sniffle.

"Please, Rinnah," she said between tiny sobs. "Give her the Royal Ruby."

Lightning flashed and Rinnah turned to look at her friends.

"That's not what she wants," she yelled over the thunder.

"Whaddya mean that's not what she wants?" Tommy yelled back. "She said to give her the ruby."

"No, she didn't," Rinnah argued. "She said to give her the Rose."

Even in the darkness, Rinnah knew her friends stared at her. Stared at her because they didn't understand.

"The Rose isn't the Royal Ruby. It never was."

More lightning, and Rinnah saw three sets of eyes bulging from their sockets.

"Reeeeenaaaaah!" Tina screamed from below. Even over the thunder, Rinnah and her friends heard her.

Rinnah shivered, but kept talking.

"The Rose isn't the Royal Ruby at all," she explained. "It's a person. The Rose is a *person*."

Tina continued wailing from the living room below the loft.

"Give me the Rose, or I'm gonna come up!"

Meagen whimpered. Rinnah laid a hand on her shoulder in an effort to calm her.

"Rinnah," Tommy yelled. "You're crazy!"

Rinnah stood and looked over the loft wall. "No, I'm not." She cocked her head down to the room below. "But Tina is."

Tommy and Meagen stood and looked over the loft wall. Lightning struck again, and they saw the Florist for the first time.

Tina had pulled the hood of the rain slicker down, and her face could clearly be seen by the flash of lightning.

"Oh my God!" Meagen backed away from the loft wall. "Tina's the Florist."

Rinnah nodded. "And she's here to kill the Rose."

"I don't get it," Tommy said. "Who *is* the Rose?"

Rinnah backed away from the loft wall and looked at her friends.

"To the medicine man and other secret-keepers of the tribe, Katharine Black Elk has another name."

Rinnah looked at the crouching girl.

"Katharine is the Rose."

THE BLOOD LINE
CHAPTER THIRTY-TWO

KATHARINE BLACK ELK stood on trembling legs.

"I don't understand..."

Rinnah looked over the loft and waited for another flash of lightning. When it came, she saw that Tina still waited there, tapping her knife against one leg.

"It's like your grandfather says. It's not the Indian blood that makes a person Indian. It's their way of life."

Katharine shook her head.

"Girl, you're just like him," she said. "Speaking in riddles."

"I know," Rinnah sighed. "It sounds weird. But that's what your grandfather believed, because of the bloodline. *Your* bloodline."

Katharine continued to look confused. Rinnah heard Meagen gasp and felt her come close.

"That's where the Queen of Varna ended up," Meagen said. "Rosebud. The reservation."

"And her daughter, the princess," Rinnah said to Katharine, "Is your great, great grandmother."

"So if Tina's the Florist," Tommy added, "Then that means she's here to take Katharine back to Varna."

Rinnah looked over the loft wall.

"Yes," Tina called. "I'm still here. I'm not leaving without her."

Rinnah stepped away from the wall.

"Problem is, Katharine won't make it back to Varna. Not if Tina has anything to say about it."

"That's right," Meagen said. "There's a whole faction of people who don't want the royalty back in Varna."

Katharine leaned against the edge of the loft.

"I just can't believe this stuff," she said. "I can't believe my grandfather would keep this from me."

Rinnah stepped toward the loft wall, next to Katharine. A flash of lightning struck and Rinnah gasped.

The living room was empty.

Just before the thunder hit, Rinnah heard the door to the loft stairway bang against the wall.

"She's coming!"

HELP!

CHAPTER THIRTY-THREE

"WE HAVE TO JUMP!" Rinnah yelled over the thunder.

"Wait for some lightning so you can see."

In the darkness, the kids felt their way onto the loft wall.

Rinnah felt another presence enter the loft just as lightning struck. She saw the sofa below her. And out of the corner of her eye, she saw the flash of a steel blade.

"Jump!"

Rinnah and her friends leapt into the darkness. After a split second of freefalling, Rinnah felt herself hit the sofa cushion.

Thunder crashed as Rinnah rolled from the sofa.

"Is everyone here?" she yelled.

Rinnah reached out into the darkness. She felt someone grasping her feet.

"It's me!" Meagen yelled.

"I'm OK!" came Katharine's voice.

"Tommy?"

No answer.

Rinnah screamed again, "Tommy! Where are you?" then listened as the thunder faded. She heard a muffled moan.

"I'm OK. I think," Tommy groaned. "But my arm hurts. Bad."

Rinnah felt through the darkness, catching hold of Meagen and Katharine. Together, the three girls moved as one to the end of the sofa.

"Here he is," Katharine called out.

Rinnah could just make out the dark outlines of the girls as they helped Tommy to his feet. They shuffled him over to one of the chairs and sat him down.

"We have to leave," Katharine said. "Let's run to my car and get out of here."

Just as Rinnah was about to agree, another bolt of lighting struck. She looked up and saw Tina standing on the edge of the loft wall. Her face contorted in rage and a snarl spewed from her mouth.

Meagen screamed.

Darkness again, and Rinnah heard a loud thump.

Tina was in the room with them.

As Rinnah went to pull Tommy to his feet, the front door opened.

Wind shrieked into the room, carrying with it sodden leaves and the cold, stinging wet of rainwater.

A figure stepped into the room. A man. Tall. Strong-looking.

"Thank God."

Rinnah turned away from him. She looked into the darkness of the living room.

Lightning flashed again, and she saw Tina leaping over the coffee table, knife blade swinging wildly in front of her.

Darkness filled the living room once again, and Rinnah threw herself over Tommy. She saw the man from the doorway run into the room.

Rinnah called out.

"Katharine! Meagen!"

She felt the girls scurry behind the chair.

With Tommy groaning in her ear, Rinnah strained to see what was happening in the living room in front of her.

She heard the crash of furniture over the swell of thunder. Pieces of something showered her as she huddled in the chair.

Another flash of lightning.

She saw Tina do a neat roundhouse kick to the figure, sending him flying into the sofa.

Darkness again. Rinnah thought that the storm must be moving on, because she heard the struggle coming from a few feet in front of her before the thunder broke.

A raging snarl from Tina, and a grunt from the man. Rinnah heard a sickening crunch and imagined a fist crashing into someone's face.

The thunder came. Rinnah waited for it to die away. When it did, she heard only the ragged sound of someone breathing.

Who was it? Tina?

Suddenly, the kitchen light flared back on, blinding Rinnah for a moment. She heard someone walk past the chair and switch on the living room's over-head light. Painful light flooded the room.

Rinnah opened her eyes and gasped.

Tina lay unconscious next to the broken coffee table.

Rinnah looked beside her and gasped.

Victor Little Horn wiped bright red blood from the corner of his mouth and spoke between gasps of breath.

"I do NOT dig chicks who kick."

SUMMER VACATION

CHAPTER THIRTY-FOUR

Rinnah huddled under a blanket next to the roaring fire and looked at the scene taking place in the cabin living room. She watched as a young man wrapped a splint around Tommy's arm. Tommy, beaming with pride, asked the paramedic, "When do I get my cast?"

After her broken nose got bandaged, Tina Treadwell was taken away in a police car.

"My own assistant," Mrs. Lane had said. "Do you think she lied on her college transcripts?"

Mr. Paige and Sandy sat on the sofa, consoling Meagen.

Rinnah smiled when she saw Sandy put her arms around the shaken girl and hold her close.

Katharine Black Elk, the Rose, continued answering questions posed by a police detective. She shook her head at every question, still not sure of what had happened. What was still happening.

"How did you know it was Katharine?"

Rinnah turned and looked Ben Forrest in the eye.

"Indian blood," she answered. Then, off of Ben's frown, she said, "Her grandfather made a big deal of Indian blood having nothing to do with being Indian. Not exactly PC, so it got me to thinking. I knew that our tribe had taken in Europeans in the past. Once I knew he had the Royal Ruby, it just kinda clicked."

Ben gazed at Katharine in silence.

"When did you find out?" Rinnah asked.

"I never did. Not for sure. But I had my suspicions."

Rinnah nodded.

"Your documentary was pretty cool."

Ben grinned a thanks.

"I guess that's what led you here, to Spearfish?"

"Yeah. I had this theory that European royalty could easily come out west and hide here. Back before the reservations, when this place still belonged to the Sioux. I noticed that the rose motif started showing up right about the time the Queen of Varna had escaped her country."

Rinnah pulled the blanket tighter around her.

"I didn't know that," she said, disappointed she hadn't uncovered that in her own investigation. She watched Katharine as her interview with the detective dragged on. She remembered something she needed to ask Ben.

"Tell me about Tina," she said.

Ben looked into the fire and breathed a heavy sigh.

"She was your girlfriend?"

Ben continued gazing into the fire.

"Well, I thought she was," he answered. "And I thought her interest in my documentary was just that of a star-struck girl. How stupid was that? All along, she was just after the Rose ... and the Royal Ruby, if she could get her hands on it."

Rinnah shifted to get closer to the fire.

"But I started to get some weird vibes when I sent flowers to her once. She totally freaked out about the roses. I backed off. Lucky for me, I guess."

Rinnah then remembered the day Lily was killed in the hospital, the same day Tina behaved so strangely in the coffee house.

"Why did you hide from me back at Common Grounds? You know, I saw you behind the book shelves."

Ben blushed and looked at his hands. "Oh, that's when Tina started to really lose it. She made me promise not to let any of you know we were dating. In her twisted mind, I guess she didn't want someone to make a connection."

Ben looked into the room, his eyes landing on a chair that sat across from him. He nodded in that direction.

"Victor never did like Tina. Said her 'Mojo' was all wrong."

Rinnah laughed and looked at Victor. He sat and scowled as a police officer interviewed him.

Ben turned his attention back to Rinnah.

"But how did you know she was the Florist?"

"That henna tattoo," Rinnah smirked. "When I found out that Lily's booth was one of those mystical, crystally ones, I wondered if she had a Henna artist. An easy phone call to the organizer of the Wild West Days confirmed that hers was the only booth where you could get henna tattoos." Then Rinnah frowned. "How totally weird is it that she chose to stop into Lily's booth? Of course, the women recognized each other, having both come from Varna and working for opposite sides."

"So the organization sent Lily to warn Ronnie about the Florist?"

"Yep. And some big, bad government people sent the Florist to capture Katharine. Seems everyone in Varna found out where to find the Rose."

Under the suspicious gaze of his new policeman friend, Victor swaggered over to Ben.

"It's late, bro," he said. "I'm ready to ditch this freak show."

Ben nodded and stood to leave. Rinnah reached around and lifted Victor's backpack.

"Don't forget this," she said. "It's what you came for in the first place, right? I'm just glad you came back for it when you did."

Victor mumbled thanks and took the heavy bag from her.

"And good luck," Rinnah offered.

"For what?" Victor shifted nervously as he swung the bag over his shoulder.

"For the high school diploma exams."

Victor grimaced and looked away. Rinnah couldn't resist teasing him just a little bit more.

"Isn't that why you've buddied up to Ben? He's your tutor, right?"

Victor ignored her and made to leave.

"I saw the books at Ben's house, Victor. It's cool. What's one more little secret?"

Victor walked away without saying another word. As he stalked past Katharine, Rinnah saw the detective punch numbers into a cell phone. She saw her chance to get Katharine alone. She stood and made her way to the girl.

"I've got something for you," Rinnah said. She pulled the beaded medicine bag from her pocket and handed it to Katharine.

"This belongs to you."

Katharine accepted the bag with a trembling hand.

"The Royal Ruby," she said.

Katharine closed her eyes and took a deep breath. She knew what was inside, and what owning it meant.

"So, what are you gonna do now?" Rinnah asked.

Katharine opened her eyes. "I don't know yet," she said. "Probably have a long talk with Grandfather, as soon as he's better." Then, almost as an afterthought, Katharine said, "I don't think it's very safe for me to go on a European vacation."

Katharine clasped the medicine bag close to her chest. She looked at Rinnah and asked, "What are *you* gonna do now?"

Rinnah thought a moment before answering.

"I'm gonna enjoy my summer vacation."

THE END